Sweet and Sour

Sweet and Sour

BY DEBBI MICHIKO FLORENCE

SCHOLASTIC PRESS / NEW YORK

All rights reserved. Published by Scholastic Press, an imprint of Scholastic Inc., *Publishers since 1920*. SCHOLASTIC, SCHOLASTIC PRESS, and associated logos are trademarks and/or registered trademarks of Scholastic Inc.

The publisher does not have any control over and does not assume any responsibility for author or third-party websites or their content.

Library of Congress Cataloging-in-Publication Data available

ISBN 978-1-338-67159-9

10 9 8 7 6 5 4 3 2 1   22 23 24 25 26

Printed in Italy   183

First edition, July 2022

Book design by Stephanie Yang

TO LISA FUNG FOR OUR LIFELONG FRIENDSHIP THAT STARTED WHEN WE WERE FOUR YEARS OLD, THROUGH UPS AND DOWNS, SO MUCH BOY DRAMA, AND COLLEGE ADVENTURES. THANK YOU FOR ALWAYS BEING THERE FOR ME.

I

Memories are funny things. They have a life of their own, bubbling up when you least expect them. And once they unfurl before your eyes, there's almost nothing you can do to stop them.

Some memories are sweet, the kind you are happy to replay in your mind. They make you smile and your heart skip. You want to curl up with those memories and snuggle them. But there are sour memories, too. Sharp, painful ones that make you flinch and your heart curdle. Like I said, you can't control the kind of memories that appear. So it's often better not to remember them at all.

Sometimes, though, it just happens. Like when the plane touched down on the runway, and I jolted awake. We were back in Mystic, Connecticut, where I'd spent six weeks of every summer for the first eleven years of my life. Two years had passed since the last time we'd come, and as I blinked at the familiar sight of TF Green Airport, I shoved the memories of previous summers down deep inside myself. I held them there as we disembarked, grabbed our luggage from one of the four baggage carousels, and climbed into the hired car waiting for us at the pickup spot. My parents laughed at how disoriented I seemed—I never fell asleep on our cross-country summer flights. But this summer was different.

I tried to look on the bright side, at how excited Mom was to see Holly, her best friend since college. Not long after graduating, Holly had married Wes Koyama and moved from California to Fairfield, Connecticut, and she and my mom had made a pact to see each other at least once a year. Fortunately the Koyama family had a vacation house in Mystic for all of us to use in the summer. Mom and Holly had kept their promise to each other until Wes's job had taken the family to Japan for two years. Last summer was the first they'd ever missed. But now they would be reunited. I grinned, thinking of my best friend back home, Lila Tan, and how our friendship would last forever like Mom and Holly's had.

"It's nice to see you smile, finally," Mom said as we drove over the border from Rhode Island into Connecticut.

"Hmmm." I didn't bother explaining to her that my smile had nothing to do with being here for the summer. Mom would get to hang out with her best friend while I would be apart from mine. I'd had to leave Lila behind in California, and that thought vaporized all my good feelings.

"Oh, Mai," Mom said, putting her arm around my shoulders and hugging me toward her. "Don't look so sad. I know you're going to miss hanging out with Lila this summer, but she'll be visiting in a few weeks. You'll see her then."

Mom was right. I blew out a breath and pasted on a smile. I knew my parents loved me, but I also knew that they didn't know how to handle it when I was sad. A memory surfaced from when I was in the third grade. A friend—or at least I'd thought she was a friend—had disinvited me from her birthday party, and I'd cried uncontrollably. When I couldn't stop, Mom had gotten frustrated with me, brushing off my sadness. To be fair, she had been in the middle of a conference call, but still.

"And," Dad said from the front passenger seat, smiling at me, "you get to spend the summer with Zach!"

Both of my parents still thought that Zach Koyama was my best friend. Because of course they did. We used to be inseparable. We'd spend every waking moment of our summers playing and talking and laughing. During the rest of the year, I'd count the days until we'd be reunited.

But all that had changed. Two summers ago, he'd humiliated me, and our friendship had shattered. Something my parents and, probably his, didn't know. If the Koyamas had come back to the States last summer instead of staying in Japan, maybe Zach and I could have fixed what had broken. But too much time had passed, and my anger had grown. All I wanted now was to punish Zach. What was that saying? Revenge was sweet, and I was definitely going to get my revenge!

As always, Dad asked the driver to take Exit 90—the scenic route—even though it meant fighting the aquarium and museum traffic. But traditions were important, and I was especially glad for this one because it would delay our arrival.

We passed motels and a gas station, a mill, and quaint (as Mom called them) New England houses totally unlike the stucco homes and townhouse communities back in Silicon Valley. I pressed my face against the window as we drove along the river, watching cormorants dive into the water.

Gradually all the anger I had for Zach was replaced by the hum of low-level excitement. I had mostly great memories of Mystic, and I'd get to spend the next six weeks doing all the things I loved—birdwatching, hiking, collecting rocks and feathers, and being in nature. But when the car made the right turn to leave the river behind, my heart squeezed in my chest. Anger battled with excitement. In the end, anger won.

The driver made a sharp turn onto Egret Pond Road, the

Koyama's private lane. I was surprised not to hear the crunch of gravel.

"Oh!" Dad exclaimed. "They paved the road."

The smooth sound of tires against asphalt was oddly foreign and jarring. Around the curve, Egret Pond came into sight, the sun sparking stars on the water's surface. At least the view was the same. The car pulled up in front of the detached garage, and I looked up at the Koyamas' three-story colonial house, my heart pounding because I'd see Zach in moments.

Memories swirled inside my head, threatening to rise to the surface. So many memories, sweet and sour, of this house and pond, the scent of lilacs and mud, the prickling heat. And Zach. Always Zach.

Dad opened the door.

"It's go-time," I said under my breath as I pushed the memories away and stepped out of the car.

2

"Mai! Mai!" Two small but powerful bodies crashed into me. Tiny arms wrapped me in a tight hug. I laughed and hugged the twins back with all my might.

When they finally let go, I squatted down. "Whoa. You two got big!"

"We're six now," Mason said proudly.

Ethan nodded. Though he was twenty minutes older, Ethan was slightly smaller than his fraternal twin but had the same inky-black hair with the Koyama cowlick in front. I'd wondered if the boys would remember me. They'd only been four when we had last been together, and I was happy they hadn't forgotten.

I stood up in time to see Holly, her long black hair in a side braid, run from the back gate into my mom's arms, the two squealing and hugging like they were still in college. It made my heart ache for missing Lila. I'd video chat her as soon as I got settled in my room.

Holly came over to greet me and Dad with hugs as the car pulled away. The boys, already tired of the reunion, took off running back to the house shouting about cookies.

"Mai! You look so grown up!" Holly said with a smile. "I love your hair down. I wish my hair was naturally wavy like that."

My eyes got misty as I followed everyone to the house. I'd missed this place. I'd missed Holly and Wes and the twins. After spending every summer here (minus the last one), this place felt like home, and the Koyamas were family.

I entered the backyard, taking in the gorgeous flowers, with honeybees flitting from bloom to bloom. The burst of colors reminded me of last night's fireworks. I'd gone to Shoreline Amphitheatre with Lila and her parents. I missed her already.

Mom and Holly talked nonstop as they circled the garden. Dad dragged all our luggage into the house through the back door.

I paused, wondering where Zach was. I hadn't planned what I'd say to him, but whatever it was it needed to be sharp and firm, to let him know he wasn't forgiven. I was surprised he hadn't come out to greet Mom and Dad at least. They were as much family to him as his parents were to me. Was he at our fort?

"Zach's not here," Holly called out to me.

"Where is he?" I asked, my hand on the screen door.

"He went back home with Wes for fireworks in Fairfield. They'll be back with some of Zach's friends tomorrow for the party."

The party. I was so focused on revenge that I'd nearly forgotten about Zach's birthday. Our summer tradition was to have his party the first weekend we were in town, and mine the last. I grimaced.

Holly misinterpreted my expression. "Don't worry, Mai. He'll be here before you know it. I know he's excited to see you."

Yeah, right.

But now that I didn't have to face Zach yet, I marched right into the house and straight up the two flights of stairs to the attic. At the top of the stairway, I pushed the door open to the room I always stayed in. My room. It was nearly three times bigger than my tiny bedroom in our Sunnyvale townhouse. Dad had already dropped off my suitcase. It stood in the middle of the rug looking a little lonely and out of place.

I let my teal corduroy tote bag slide off my shoulder with a thump onto the wood floor and breathed a huge sigh of relief. Nothing had changed.

Early evening sunlight streamed in from the windows as I peered out at Egret Pond. Mom and Dad's bedroom was directly below mine, and in typical Koyama generosity, we had the best views. Mine was even better than my parents' because, on the third floor, my windows sat well above the treetops, giving me a clear view of the pond, the apple orchard, and the garage. I couldn't see it from here, but our fort was just beyond the garage near the pond. Perfect for birdwatching.

As much as I wanted to go check it out, it would be dinner soon. Plus, we'd do the usual gift exchange between the families. I was excited to see what Holly had brought from Japan. The fort would have to wait till tomorrow. I'd wake up early and sneak out there before Zach and his friends arrived.

I wandered through my room, running my fingers across the desktop and stopping at the bookcase where my rabbit collection was displayed. Rabbits have always been my favorite, and every year for my birthday, the Koyamas would get me a new figurine. I grabbed my tote bag from the floor and peered at the pink rabbit plush keychain hanging off the strap. Lila had given it to me last night. We both stanned BTS, and Cooky was the BT21 character for my bias, Jungkook. Lila had a matching tote bag in pink with a Chimmy plush keychain for her bias, Jimin.

The aroma of grilled salmon wafted up to my room. My stomach rumbled. I'd unpack later when I called Lila. I ran down the stairs, smiling, my heart feeling light.

Dinner was on the screened-in back porch, where we always gathered for meals. It was the perfect place to enjoy Holly's delicious cooking without worrying about mosquitoes nipping at our legs. Holly had always loved to cook, but while in Japan, she'd taken classes and had really upped her game.

After dinner, we moved to the living room for our gift exchange. Mom and Holly had it down to a science and were able to drag it out for an hour or longer. But as much as I loved this tradition, it felt a little wrong to be doing it without Zach and his dad.

The twins got plenty of gifts, which they tore into with the excitement of kids whose birthdays were still half a year away. But after a while, they started getting squirmy watching the adults ooh and aah over scarves, plates, and tea (from Holly) and chocolate, hats, and sourdough bread (from us).

"And, of course, we didn't forget you, Mai," Holly said, handing me a bag.

"Umeboshi!" I exclaimed, pulling out a container of pickled plums, my favorite.

Ethan scrunched his nose. "Ew!"

"Not a fan?" I asked him, waving the jar in his face. Japanese pickled plums were tart and salty and perfect with rice, but I also loved eating them right out of the jar. Saliva pooled in my mouth just thinking about the taste of ume.

"Ethan has a sweet tooth like Zach," Holly said, ruffling Ethan's hair.

Holly had also gotten me a bag of ume candy. I popped a piece in my mouth, and at first, all I could taste was pure sugar, but as soon as the hard candy dissolved, I was left with a burst of sourness from the ume in the center. "This is fab! Thank you!"

The rest of my gift bag contained a scarf with a pretty cherry blossom print and a bunch of cute bunny trinkets and stickers. As Holly started telling my mom about her favorite shops in Tokyo, I excused myself and slipped upstairs.

When I finally got back to my room, I called Lila, grinning when her face came into view.

"I miss you!" she said with a spin of her drumsticks. She wasn't allowed to carry them around in school, but at home, they were always in her tote bag or in her hands.

"Same." I felt tears prick my eyes, and I blinked quickly to keep them from escaping.

"So?" she prompted.

I shook my head. "He won't be here till tomorrow."

We fell immediately into our favorite game: listing our ideas for revenge.

"Shave off his eyebrows," Lila said.

"Toss his video games into the pond," I answered.

"Burn his favorite shirt."

"Dump a nest of spiders in his bed."

"Post an embarrassing pic of him on Instagram." Lila held her drumsticks up in an X.

Then we rolled our eyes. That would definitely not be possible. Both of our parents had rules, and one was no social media until high school. One more year to go. Besides, as far as I knew Zach wasn't on social media, either.

We moved on to Lila's plans for getting her band together. First practice for the Hot Pinx started tomorrow. Her dad had soundproofed the garage as much as possible, and so far, none of the neighbors had complained about her drumming.

"Everyone's in?" I asked. Lila had recruited members from the after-school band club.

Lila nodded. "Me on drums, of course. Iris Yamaguchi on vocals, Quinn Henderson on guitar, and Alex Garcia on bass."

"Woot! Your plan worked!" I teased. "A powerful all-girl band, plus Alex." Lila had had a crush on Alex all through seventh grade.

She blushed. "Well, not for nothing, Alex *is* the best bass player."

"Of course. Only the best for the Hot Pinx," I said.

"I wish you could join us."

I laughed. "I don't play an instrument, and I can't sing."

"But you dance like a queen," Lila said.

That I did.

"This feels weird," she said. "Being apart."

I nodded. We'd met in homeroom in sixth grade and quickly became BFFs. Last summer we'd spent all our time together, literally. Sleepovers every weekend. We were both only children, but meeting Lila had felt like gaining a sister.

"But you'll be here in a few weeks," I said.

"And I'll help you get the ultimate revenge against the Evil One," Lila said, doing an air rimshot with her drumsticks.

"Mai! Mai!" Mason barreled into my room. "Tuck us in! Read us a book!"

"I have to go," I said to Lila. "Talk tomorrow? After your band practice?"

"Definitely." She held out a pinkie to the screen.

I did the same, and we said, "Stay gold," before logging off.

Mason grabbed my hand and dragged me across the narrow hall to Zach's room. This was new.

"You're sharing a room with Zach?" I asked.

"Yes!" Ethan shouted from his bed. "We're big boys now!"

Two summers ago, the twins had slept in their parents' room. I wondered how Zach felt about sharing. But then maybe it didn't matter much since we spent all our time in our fort. Or at least we used to.

"Read to us!" Ethan commanded as Mason climbed onto his own twin mattress. Their beds were on the opposite side of Zach's in the large room. Like mine, Zach's bed was tucked under the sloping eaves of the attic ceiling. We used to keep score of how many times each of us banged our heads on the ceiling over the summer.

I scanned Zach's side. While my room hadn't changed, Zach's was nothing like I remembered. It wasn't only that Ethan and Mason had moved in. There was also a table and chairs in the middle of the room, an in-progress LEGO project stacked upon it. New posters on the wall had replaced the Nintendo and race car ones I was used to. One showed a Japanese girl staring intensely at the camera, a red cloth draped over half of her face. The other poster was of a band called vivid undress, no capital letters. The girl from the first poster was on this one, too, the only girl among the four other band members. She was pretty.

"Zach loves Kiila," Ethan sang, bouncing on his bed in his jammies.

"Daisukidesu," Mason chimed in, his Japanese sounding perfect. I couldn't speak or understand, but I knew that meant "I like you" or "I love you," depending on the speaker's intention.

Wow. I hadn't thought of it before, but the boys were probably fluent in Japanese now. Did Zach speak Japanese, too? It looked like he was into Japanese bands. And girls.

I hadn't even seen him yet, and he already seemed different. As much as I was angry at him and looked forward to getting him back for disrespecting me, I still wanted him to be the same Zach I'd known all my life.

"Mai!" Mason interrupted my thoughts.

"Okay," I said. "Let's read."

As I turned away from Zach's side of the room, my gaze wandered from the posters and caught on something familiar on his nightstand.

He still had the flashlight.

Sweet

FOUR SUMMERS AGO

"Arggghhhh!"

At that unexpected yowl in the middle of the night, I bolted up in bed and conked my head on the low ceiling. That made seven times so far this summer, two ahead of Zach.

"Oh my God! Amai! Where are you?"

So, it wasn't a bad dream. I rubbed my eyes and slid out of bed, careful to keep my head low. Even though I was eight years old and small for my age, the ceiling was so sharply sloped that I had to duck or I'd hit my head again.

In the dim moonlight shining through the windows, I made my way across the room, the ceiling fan wafting warm air in swirls behind me as I crossed the hall.

"Zach?" I peered into my best friend's room.

"What took you so long?" Zach's voice was thin and reedy with fear. "I could have been murdered by now!"

I reached over and flipped on the light. Zach was curled up at the foot of his bed.

"What's up?" I asked as we both blinked until our eyes had adjusted.

"I felt something in my hair." Zach scrubbed his head furiously, making his cowlick even more obvious. He was a year older than me, but I'd always been braver.

I walked over and squinted past him at the wall. "It was probably that spider," I said, pointing.

Zach screamed and threw his pillow at it. Fortunately he missed.

"Don't do that," I said. "You'll hurt it! It's not doing anything to you."

"It's in my room! It's trespassing! Plus, spiders bite!" Zach tumbled backward off his bed with a thump onto the hardwood floor. He was wearing his purple-and-yellow basketball shorts and a red Mario Kart T-shirt, clashing as usual. He had the worst fashion sense ever. His parents let him dress himself, but I always felt like they should at least help him match colors.

I climbed onto his bed to rescue the spider, but it had disappeared. "I don't see it anymore," I said.

"What? NOOOO!" Zach leapt to his feet, holding his hands to his head.

"Yup, it's gone." I crawled off the bed, keeping low to protect my head. "Go back to sleep."

"It's not gone! It's hiding. It might be in my bed!"

I grabbed the covers and shook them. "Nothing."

"*In* my bed," he whispered.

I yanked off the thin blanket and his top sheet. "There's no spider, Zach."

"Then it's under my bed!"

I got down on my hands and knees and peered beneath the bedframe. "It's too dark to tell. I'm sure it's going to leave you alone."

When I straightened, there was Zach sitting in the middle of his room, knees to his chest, chin on his knees, wide-eyed. His hair stuck up in clumps. Somehow in the last year, Zach had become terrified of spiders. I wouldn't abandon him when he'd always looked out for me. Friends protected each other. Zach had taught me that.

"Don't move," I said as I left his room.

Back in mine, I grabbed the flashlight that I used for nighttime excursions from my closet. Never mind that last summer our parents forbade us from leaving the house at night without permission. We'd gone outside at midnight because Zach had wanted to see the stars and I'd wanted to catch a bullfrog. They croaked so loudly at night. Holly had not been happy when she'd come to get us at the pond in her nightgown. New rules, but it wouldn't stop us from exploring at least.

I returned to find Zach in the same position I'd left him. So I turned on my flashlight and crawled back under his bed, sweeping the light around. "Aha!" The spider was creeping along the baseboard. "Get me a piece of paper," I said, hoping Zach wasn't frozen with fear.

A few seconds later, he shoved a magazine in my hand. I scooted on my belly and nudged the magazine at the spider. It took some convincing, but once it finally crawled onto the cover of *Electronic Gaming Monthly*, I slowly backed up until we were both out from under the bed.

"Kill it!" Zach said when I stood up.

"No way." I walked carefully over to his window and pushed it open. The sweet scent of roses mixed with salt air wafted in. Then I tilted the magazine so the spider could crawl onto the outside ledge. "You're safe now," I told Zach as I closed the window.

"But what if he has friends and family?" Zach's brown eyes flitted around his room.

I spent the next hour crawling around the floor and standing on chairs with my flashlight, scouring Zach's room for intruders. When he was finally convinced that his room was bug free, we both collapsed on top of his bed, the covers on the floor where I'd tossed them.

"Thanks, Amai," Zach whispered sleepily. "You're my hero."

"I *am* pretty awesome," I said, yawning, right before we both fell asleep.

3

By the time I woke up the next morning, the summer sun had warmed my room enough that I was sweating and sticking to my sheets. The only drawback to the attic bedroom was the heat. Wes usually put in the window AC units when the heat got unbearable later in July, so for now I relied upon the ceiling fan and another one standing in the corner, both of which I'd forgotten to turn on last night. Once the twins had fallen asleep, I'd snuck over to Zach's side of the room. My old flashlight still had a piece of masking tape on it with Zach's neat printing spelling out *Amai's Spider Light*.

I glanced at the time on my phone. It was ten o'clock! So much for waking up early. It always took me a few days to get used to the new time zone. I showered quickly, and as I dried off, I noticed Zach's towel hanging from the rack. Maybe I could buy itching powder online. Shaking my head, I thought, *That's too light a punishment.* Zach deserved to feel embarrassed the way I'd felt embarrassed, to hurt the way I hurt. Even so, before I left the bathroom, I yanked his towel off the rack and let it fall into a heap on the floor.

Back in my room, I changed into my favorite floral-print dress, one with deep pockets for stones and feathers and other treasures. Then I scurried down the two flights of stairs and found everyone sitting on the screened porch. Dad raised his coffee mug to me as the boys pounced on me.

"Did you and Mom sleep in?" I asked, hugging the Twin Tornadoes. Zach had dubbed them that because they left a wake of destruction wherever they went.

"Holly and I went for a morning bike ride," Mom said.

As I sat down and grabbed a croissant, Dad stood, his chair scraping against the wood floor. "You boys ready?"

"Yes!" Ethan and Mason shouted.

"You want to come with us?" Dad asked me. "We're going to pick up a few things for Zach's party and then stop for ice cream downtown."

Downtown. I hadn't been there since the end of our last summer in Mystic. I slapped the memory of that humiliating day down before it could take over my thoughts.

"I'll stay," I said.

Holly glanced at her phone. "Looks like Wes will be here with Zach and his friends soon."

"Okay." I shoved the rest of the flaky pastry in my mouth and excused myself from the table. I didn't need to say where I was heading. Everyone knew.

Nabbing the key hanging at the back door, I slid on my gray Converse slip-ons. We had to remove our shoes in the house, and with the way I came and went, these were the best shoes. Zach had always worn ratty flip-flops, which surprised me for someone so freaked out about bugs.

I scooted out the back gate and crossed the wide driveway to the lawn and then through the apple orchard. Mom's and Holly's matching hammocks were already strung between the trees. As I followed the familiar path around the side of the garage and along the pond, the fort came into view, and my heart soared. Of everything I'd lost while the Koyamas had been in Japan, I'd missed our fort the most.

I ran the rest of the way, stopping at the door to gaze up fondly at our sign.

Fort Amazuppai. That was our parents' nickname for Zach and me. It meant "sweet and sour" in Japanese. Even though Zach was only a year and a month older than me, from the time I could crawl we had been inseparable. But we were also complete opposites. Two forces of nature that balanced each other out. I'd always teased

Zach that he was the sour one—after all, Amai literally meant "sweet."

Zach was the only one who still called me by my full first name.

I ran my finger over the worn sign. The summer the twins were born, Wes and my dad had built this cabin for me and Zach to give us our very own space. The first time we opened the door to our fort, Zach made a rule. Nobody but the two of us could ever step foot into Fort Amazuppai. Sometimes we were forced to make an exception for our parents, but they rarely came by.

I unlocked the door and flipped on the lights. The Koyamas had arrived here in late June, but even though Zach had already been to our fort, I knew all my things would be untouched. We respected each other's space. Plus, Zach was completely grossed out by my collection of feathers, bones, and molted cicada shells.

"I missed you," I said out loud.

Zach's orange beanbag chair sat in the corner next to a trunk that probably still held all the old Game Boy cartridges he'd abandoned for a Nintendo Switch. His bookshelf was lined with well-read manga and graphic novels, along with the Funko Pop figures he'd been collecting forever, mostly of Marvel characters. Nothing had changed in here.

Or at least that's what I thought until I noticed a whole row of books I didn't recognize. Travel books! Not only for Japan, but for

Korea, Vietnam, Australia, Spain, and others. And now that I was looking, there were framed photos of places in Japan on Zach's wall. Those were new, too. Now he was some kind of world traveler or something?

I faced his beanbag chair and squared my shoulders as I thought about what I'd say to Zach when I finally saw him.

"You don't belong here," I said, making my voice hard.

No. That wasn't quite right. I mean, it was his parents' house and property after all. I cleared my throat and tried again.

"You don't deserve to hang out in this fort anymore. It's only for loyal friends."

That wasn't quite the burn I was hoping for, either.

"I wish you'd stayed in Japan and never come back!"

That was better. Not perfect, but it'd show Zach how much he'd messed up. Maybe I'd lead with that. Anger smoldered in my stomach. As soon as I got my revenge, maybe I could let it go.

On my side of the fort, wireless speakers hung from the corners of the ceiling. I resisted the urge to put on my favorite playlist. I wouldn't be dancing here this summer for sure.

The wood bench Wes had made for me still sat in front of a big window that faced the pond. I lifted the bench seat and was happy to see my binoculars and birding notebook.

A small bookshelf held my nature collection: stones and shells and feathers and, of course, my bird books, including my cherished Sibley's Guide. Zach made fun of how many books I had, but every single one was different and worn with use. They helped me identify specific birds like hawks and owls, or species local to Connecticut. I flipped through the curling pages of my waterfowl guide, which was water stained from the time I'd dropped it at the pond's edge.

I plopped down on the bench with the Connecticut bird book. Just as I was about to lift my binoculars to my face, I heard the door open, and my heart slammed into my chest so hard it hurt.

I wasn't ready to see Zach. I hadn't come up with the perfect insult yet or figured out how to make him pay for hurting me. I had nothing but a twisting stomach and a simmering hate for the boy I'd once thought was my forever best friend.

I looked up to see a stranger standing in the doorway. She had peacock-blue eyes and sparrow-brown hair that fell in waves past her shoulders, and her denim cutoffs and pink tank top showed off golden skin. I observed all this in one lightning-quick glance. Years of birdwatching had trained me to take in details quickly.

"Hello, Mai," she said with a smile. "I'm Celeste. Zach's friend, Celeste Williams? He's bringing our bags into the house, but he told me you'd be here."

I gritted my teeth. Zach had invited another person into our fort. Once again, he'd disrespected his own rule.

Sour

TWO SUMMERS AGO

Zach had gone to run errands with his dad while I played with the twins. At four years old, they were already a handful but adorable. We were in the middle of having a dinosaur battle—Mason's Stegosaurus was trouncing my T. rex. Ethan was building a wall out of sticks around his Triceratops.

"Naptime," Holly called from the back door.

Ethan and Mason hugged me before running to their mom. I tossed the dinosaurs into a plastic bucket and brought them into the house. Then I grabbed Mom's iPad. Even though I was about to turn eleven, she said I was still too young to have my own.

In the fort, I propped the iPad up on my bookcase and cued up my favorite dance practice video, "Boy With Luv" by BTS. I pulled my shoulders back, anticipating the opening chords and counting in my head so I could flip back my imaginary coat at the exact right moment. I moved my shoulders, leaning left, then right, and I lost myself in the dance. My arms tingled as I hopped around the floor, my smile growing with each step. I felt like I was flying. Zach had cheered me on all summer as I practiced the moves until I had the choreography down perfectly.

As the video came to an end, I hit Jungkook's final pose. I grinned to myself and thought I'd run through it again when a burst of applause made me gasp and spin around.

There in the doorway was Zach and two white boys I'd never seen before. How long had they been there? Zach and I had a very strict rule. Fort Amazuppai was for us and only us. No visitors. No siblings. No friends.

"That was amazing!" Zach exclaimed. "You nailed it!"

I smiled. "You think?" My head felt light, but I wasn't sure if it was because of Zach's praise or that I was embarrassed having two strangers watch me dance.

"Definitely!"

Zach stepped in and the boys followed. While they looked around, I studied them from the corner of my eye. Relieved they weren't looking at me anymore, I didn't have to fake a smile. I could tell they were brothers. The older one looked like he might be a teenager, and the younger one looked about

Zach's age. They both had dirty-blond hair buzzed short.

I shot Zach a look, and he had the decency to look guilty.

"I met Ryder and Colt at the hardware store," he said. "They're here on vacation for the rest of the week."

"Hey," Colt, the younger one, said.

Ryder ignored me as he rummaged through Zach's trunk. Rude! He'd just met Zach, and he was already way too comfortable in our space. I grabbed Mom's iPad and hugged it to me, eyeing Zach warily. We'd been friends long enough that I didn't have to say a word to let him know how I felt about this.

"Let's go look at the pond," Zach suggested suddenly.

"Sure. Whatever. This place is boring." Ryder had moved over to Zach's shelves. He dropped the Mario and Luigi figures he'd been scrutinizing onto the floor. "C'mon," he said, shoving Colt toward the door.

Zach glanced at me but said nothing as he followed them. The click of the door latching closed made my stomach sink.

Grabbing the toys Ryder had so callously tossed, I put them back on the shelf where they belonged. A heaviness blanketed the fort. To try to shake off the weird energy, I started to pace. What should I do with myself now? I definitely didn't feel like dancing anymore. But there was no way I was going to hang out with those boys. I didn't understand why Zach had brought them over. It was supposed to be our place and no one else's. And we only had a couple of weeks left of summer to enjoy it. Hopefully this was a one-time thing, and I'd get Zach to myself again.

Finally I gave up pacing, locked the door behind me, and headed back to the house, my afternoon in the fort totally soured.

4

It seemed Zach still couldn't follow his own rule.

His friend Celeste smiled and as much as I wanted to tell her to get out, I couldn't be rude. It wasn't her fault.

"Hi," I said, trying not to grit my teeth. "I'll just be a minute."

At least she hadn't come barging in. While she waited at the door, I put my things away, then stepped into the bright summer sun, pulling the door shut behind me.

As we walked the path back toward the house, Celeste peppered me with questions.

"Are you excited for Zach's party?"

"Do you love this pond?"

"Are there a lot of mosquitoes out?"

She didn't leave space for me to answer, which was fine since I was still trying to wrap my head around her unexpected appearance at the fort.

Suddenly Celeste's monologue was interrupted by a deep-voiced shout. "Amai!"

I blinked, expecting Wes to round the corner. But only Zach called me that.

Someone who looked vaguely like him but taller than I remembered ran toward us at full speed. I didn't have to time to prepare. He slammed into me on the pathway, and as he wrapped me in a hug, the familiar scent of coconut shampoo enveloped me.

I closed my eyes. *Zach.* That smell took me right back to summer mornings, lying side by side under the apple trees, listening to birdsong while discussing our daily plans. Comfort and peace misted me like a gentle rain. But then the memory of Zach's betrayal burst in my head like a flash of lightning, and I was brought back to the present and who Zach really was.

The imprint of his arms seared my flesh. The hug was so unexpected and shocking that my brain seized, making me forget how to move my limbs. Not that I would have hugged him back. In all the times I'd fantasized about our reunion, a hug had never once entered my thoughts. It was over in an instant, but still, it left me breathless. As Zach pulled away, I saw the hurt in his eyes.

He recovered quickly and turned to point to a small group of people behind him. In the deep voice I hadn't recognized, he made introductions. "Noah Murdocca, Owen Mitchell, Evan Hall, Jesse

Diaz, and Bennett Morris. And you met Celeste. Everyone, this is Mai."

There was a chorus of friendly greetings. I was the only one who stayed quiet. I couldn't get the hug out of my head. And I couldn't believe how Zach's voice had changed. I was incapable of a snappy or snide comment, much less a coherent greeting.

Zach had been back in the States since March, and I had wondered how hard it must have been to finish eighth grade in Fairfield after being away. But as I watched Zach laugh and joke with his friends, I guessed it hadn't been too bad since he had people to invite to his party. He and Noah had been friends since elementary school. Maybe they'd kept in touch while Zach was away. Zach and I never communicated between summers.

"Zachary Koyama!" Holly's voice carried. "Did you really leave these bags in the middle of the hallway?"

"Oops! We'd better head back," Zach said. He led the way, and his friends followed. Celeste, the only girl in the group, walked next to me.

I belatedly kicked myself for missing a prime opportunity to get back at Zach. He couldn't hide the flash of hurt on his face when I hadn't returned his hug or his enthusiasm. I could have used that. Shoving him away in front of his friends or making some comment about the smell of his hair (never mind that I liked it) would have been the ultimate humiliation.

I glanced at the girl walking next to me and then at the group of boys ahead of us. As much as I wanted to embarrass Zach, I didn't know these people. No, the perfect revenge would be shaming him the way he had shamed me without the world knowing I was behind it. I only needed Zach to know it.

"Ohmigod," Celeste said, breaking into my thoughts. "Zach has talked nonstop about you."

"He has?"

"Totally! It's Mai this, Mai that." Celeste giggled, her laughter musical like a bird trill. "We call it *The Mai Show.*"

Well, that was surprising. And weird.

"It's great to meet you finally! And you and Zach have been forever friends? That's awesome sauce!" Celeste said, not seeming to notice or care that I hadn't answered yet. "I moved to Connecticut from Arizona last year. Zach and Noah and the guys have been so nice."

Celeste talked a lot. Not that I minded since I couldn't think of anything to say. By the time we made it back to the driveway, I knew she loved retro '80s rock and movies, hated reality TV, had a mint-green-and-lilac bedroom, read mystery books, and had an older sister majoring in industrial design at Georgia Tech.

For lunch, the Koyamas had set up a canopy tent on the lawn over a long table filled with food, mostly sandwiches and bowls of chips. There were a lot of bowls.

Zach turned to explain. "I brought back lots of different chip flavors from Japan and saved them for the party."

The guys made a beeline for the food, quickly filling paper plates with sandwiches and chips and potato salad until they practically overflowed. They reminded me a little of those cartoons that showed swarms of locusts devastating farm fields.

By the time Celeste and I made it to the table, there wasn't much left to choose from. Celeste took a veggie sandwich, and I snagged the last chicken and avocado. As we made our way down the table, we grabbed handfuls of all the different chips.

Zach and his friends sat under a cluster of apple trees with their plates balanced on their laps.

"Do you want to sit on the porch?" I asked Celeste. "We could eat at the table."

"Like civilized beings! Sure," she said with an easy smile.

I led her over to where my parents and Zach's, along with the twins, were finishing up. We made small talk as they gathered their empty plates and got up to make room for us. Then they headed into the yard.

At least having Celeste with me didn't make it obvious I was avoiding Zach. The last thing I wanted was for the parents to notice I was angry at him. When we were younger and got into fights, they'd make a big deal of having Peace Talks to get us to make up. I did not want to have any kind of Peace Talk with Zach. I didn't want to talk to him at all.

Celeste took a bite of one of the chips. "Ohmigod! That is vile!" She scrunched her nose. "What flavor are these?"

I nibbled the chip on my plate that looked like hers. Before I could tell her it tasted like shrimp, she popped up and ran off the porch. I watched as she sprinted over to the guys and stopped in front of Zach, her hands on her hips. He looked up at her and laughed, pointing to the table. She dashed over there, and before I knew it, she was back, sitting down next to me and tossing an array of empty chip bags on the table.

"Shrimp, beef and wasabi, seaweed, fish eggs, and something called pickled plum!" She stuck her tongue out. "Disgusting!"

Well, that was racist. An ugly memory tried to surface, but I shoved it down. I did not want this summer ruined like that last one.

"Maybe to you," I said, trying hard not to snap at her, "but obviously not to millions of Japanese people."

"Oh! I'm sorry!" Celeste grabbed my arm. "That came off totally racist." She looked genuinely ashamed. At least she apologized. That was something. I let it go. This time.

"Which one is the pickled plum?" I asked. "I love umeboshi."

Celeste riffled through the bags and handed me a pink one. I examined the photo and then searched my plate for the matching one. I crunched on the chip. "This is it!" That lip-puckering sour flavor mixed with the saltiness of the chip was so good! I ate the rest quickly.

To her credit, Celeste picked up the same chip and nibbled at it. "Hmm. Not quite my thing," she said.

"I'll eat yours."

As I devoured her ume chips, Celeste said, "You're so lucky to have known Zach your entire life."

"You think?" I totally did not feel lucky about that at all.

"I've moved five times in thirteen years. I haven't had a friend for longer than a year or two. And I've never had a best friend."

Well, that was sad. "Why do you move so often?"

"My mom's job is to open new offices for the company she works for, so she gets transferred a lot. But we always move to boring places and never out of the country like Zach got to do."

The Koyamas had been so happy when Wes got the offer to work from the Tokyo office for two years. Zach had never been anywhere outside the US before. And Holly hadn't been to Japan since college. So it was decided. It would be good for the kids to experience living in another country and connect to their heritage.

I was glad both of my parents had jobs that not only allowed us to stay put but also gave us the freedom to spend six weeks of every summer here in Mystic.

"What do your parents do?" Celeste asked, practically reading my mind.

"My mom helps schools set up new tech. And my dad"—I paused—"is Ty Hirano."

"What?" Celeste screeched. "As in the Teen Time Trekkers graphic novels?"

"Yep."

It was weird having a dad who was kind of famous. He'd illustrated book covers and picture books, and done some graphic design work my whole life. Then, two years ago, his first graphic novel was published, and it was a big hit. Good thing he had the second in the series mostly done by the time the first one hit the bestseller list, but now he was on a tight deadline for the third book.

"Wow!" Celeste looked around for my dad. "Will you introduce me? Maybe I can come back later this summer and get him to sign my books?"

"Sure."

"Do you have a best friend?" Celeste asked. I was relieved that she didn't go on and on about my dad. Not that I wasn't proud of him. I was, and I loved his books, but it felt weird when people gushed about him. I mean, to me he was just Dad.

"I do. Lila Tan." I smiled thinking of her. "She's coming to visit at the end of the month."

"You're so lucky! How did you two meet?"

"It was the first day of sixth grade in homeroom. We'd been standing kind of close to each other and we're both Asian, so I think the teacher assumed we knew each other and sat us together." I made a face. "For the first couple of days, we didn't acknowledge each other or talk to each other at all."

Celeste nodded.

"But by the third day, I recognized that Lila was just as offended as I was by the teacher making that assumption. Like just because we're both Asian we must be friends? It was then I knew I'd like her. We started talking, and I discovered she has the same sense of justice that I do. Turned out we had a lot of things in common."

"Nice. And then you became besties?" Celeste shrugged. "Sorry for all the questions. I just like to hear best friend stories, since, you know, I don't have one." She didn't say it like she wanted pity or anything. Just very matter of fact. She was open and honest and easy to like.

"It wasn't until maybe two weeks later," I said, answering her question. "I'd been walking to my locker when I saw two girls talking to Lila in the hall. Lila looked upset. When I got closer, I heard one of the girls snarkily telling Lila to pick one instrument and stick to it." I rolled my eyes. "Lila is an uber-talented musician.

She can pick up any instrument and in days play like an expert. She was annoying people in her orchestra class apparently."

"Got it," Celeste said.

"I hate it when people are mean but especially if they are being mean to a friend. Friends look out for each other."

Celeste nodded hard. "Definitely. Loyalty above all else! I totally agree."

"Anyway, I marched up to those girls and told them off. I think Lila was just as surprised as they were. They backed off, and that's when Lila and I became best friends forever."

"Awesome sauce!" Celeste said. "I hope I have a friend like that someday."

"I hope you do, too." And I meant it.

"Gift time!" Holly called from the tent. The guys whooped and ran over to the table, which was now covered in brightly wrapped presents.

"What did you get Zach?" Celeste asked as she and I walked over to the tent.

"No clue."

Zach and I never got each other presents. Our parents handled that every year. Every year, except that last one.

Sweet

TWO SUMMERS AGO

I could already smell that the grill was fired up as Zach closed the door to our fort and we started walking back to the house. He'd asked for burgers for his twelfth birthday party dinner. Mom, Dad, and I had only arrived two days earlier, and my stomach was still on California time, so I wasn't hungry yet. It didn't matter because Zach would finish whatever I left on my plate anyway.

"I have an announcement," Zach said when we joined our families. Our parents turned to listen, but the twins, who were four, continued racing around the backyard, squirting each other with water guns. "I'm postponing my birthday!"

"What?" Wes nearly dropped the burger he was flipping. "What are you talking about?"

Holly smiled. "Should we throw out your presents, then?"

"I didn't say I was skipping it. I'm trading with Amai."

It was my turn to say, "What?"

"Check it," Zach said. "You always complain how we're never the same age, so if we trade birthdays, we'll both be twelve at the same time."

Wes shook his head. "You know that's not how it works."

"Yeah, but we can pretend by switching our birthdays up."

"I wish you had suggested this before today, Zach," Holly said. She was usually up for anything. "Everything is already set up for your party. It's a sweet thought, though."

The adults went back to preparing dinner. Zach groaned and dragged his feet over to the steps of the back porch. I followed.

"That was super nice of you, Zach," I said, sitting down next to him.

"Parents ruin everything."

"It doesn't matter," I said. "It's the thought that counts, right? Besides, that's what I used to wish when I was like seven. It's not a big deal to me anymore that we're not the same age."

"Okay," he said good-naturedly. "I only thought of it like an hour ago anyway."

We both laughed. Zach wasn't known for being a planner.

"What really matters," I said, "is that you were trying to do something sweet for me. Thanks."

"Well, even though we're not switching birthdays, I have a gift for you."

I straightened. "You do?" Zach had never given me a gift himself before. I put out both my hands. "Gimme!"

Zach laughed, his eyes crinkling at the corners. "Wow. Way to be chill."

"Since when do we hide our feelings from each other?" I wiggled my fingers.

Zach dug into his front pocket, and for a brief moment, I was afraid he was going to pull out a linty piece of candy. Instead he placed something tiny and cold in the palm of my hand.

I peered at it. "A rabbit charm!" I gasped. "It's perfect! Thank you!"

"Look at the back," Zach said, sounding pleased with himself.

I flipped the charm over, and my heart fluttered like humming-bird wings. "You had it engraved?" On the back was a tiny letter *A*.

"I know you like rabbits and all," Zach said. "But see how this one is leaping? It looks like it's dancing. It reminds me of you."

For some reason, that made me feel suddenly shy. Clutching the bunny in the hug I wanted to give Zach, I said, "Thank you!"

I strung it on a piece of string and wore it around my wrist for the rest of the summer, a symbol of the tight bond we had as best friends.

I would wear it forever.

5

While Zach opened his gifts, I sat apart from the group on a lawn chair. Not far enough away to be antisocial—Mom would definitely notice that. I just didn't want to be in the middle of things. To pretend to be happy around Zach.

This was my first opportunity to get a good look at him. He seemed different—older for sure. I mean of course he seemed older; it'd been two years. He was definitely taller than me now, still on the thin side, and slightly gangly like a puppy growing into his limbs. And he must've worn braces while he was in Japan. I'd always loved the adorable gap between his two front teeth, but now it was gone.

Oh, and his clothes! I didn't know if Zach had dressed up special for the party, but his outfit made him look like a K-pop idol. He rocked faded jeans with frayed holes at both knees, a long lavender

T-shirt, and Timberlands. I wasn't used to seeing him in real shoes.

But it wasn't what he looked like that threw me the most. It was that hug. Was he putting on an act in front of his friends? Or did he really think we were still best friends?

My fists squeezed at the thought, so tightly that my nails dug into my palms, leaving little crescent indentations that would remind me to stay angry all day. Our friendship was dead. I hadn't talked to Zach in what felt like hours, but since he was surrounded by his friends, it didn't seem like he noticed.

As Zach tore through some wrapping paper to reveal a new set of Nintendo Switch Joy-Cons, he smiled and laughed. It looked like he was still into video games at least.

"Amai!" he shouted, waving the box in the air. "We can play Mario Kart!"

Um, no. I scowled. The corner of Zach's mouth twitched in surprise. He didn't miss a beat and picked up the last gift on the table. But I knew him well, and my reaction had hit its mark.

This gift was wrapped in silver paper I recognized. It was from our family. Zach ripped into it and lifted out a backpack. I crinkled my nose. We got him something for school? Boring. But judging by Zach's expression, he thought it was a great gift.

"No way!" he shouted, grinning.

"Is that the Osprey daypack?" Noah asked.

"The hydration reservoir is awesome!" Zach pulled out another thing from the box. He turned to me. "Thanks, Amai!"

My parents were watching, so this time I smiled at him and nodded. Zach used to love to hike. I guess he still did. That was reassuring.

While we all helped Holly clean up the tent, Wes set up some wood boards with holes in them in the driveway.

"Cornhole!" Celeste cheered. She ran over to me and grabbed my arm. "Me and Mai against Noah and Zach!"

"Wait! What is this?" I asked as Celeste literally dragged me to the driveway.

She did a double take. "You've never played cornhole?"

"I don't even know what that is."

Celeste explained the simple rules. We'd each try to toss four beanbags into the holes of our opponent's board. If a bag fell in a hole we would get three points. Landing on the board was one point. Whichever team got to twenty-one first won.

Zach's friends stood on the sidelines. They whooped when Celeste sunk a bag into the hole, then jeered and laughed when Noah overshot and his beanbag missed the board completely. When it was my turn, I picked up a purple bean bag. Then held my breath as I made my first toss.

As it sailed through the air, landing on the board but missing the hole, I noticed something weird: Zach was cheering for me. We were opponents! Who cheered for the opposing team? We continued alternating turns. Once I was able to shut out Zach, I ended up having fun. Especially because I sunk my next two shots. When Celeste and I won, she gave me a high five.

"We destroyed the boys!" she crowed. Then she looked over at the rest of Zach's friends. "All right, who thinks they stand a chance against the cornhole masters?"

After we lost the second match, I sat on Mom's hammock to watch as everyone took a turn playing. When the tournament was finally over, Celeste ran over to Noah and grabbed his hand. Ah, Celeste and Noah were together. They made a cute couple. She whispered something in his ear and then made her way over to me, sitting down on Holly's hammock.

"Hey, Noah and I were talking, and I think we'll be back next weekend," Celeste said tentatively. "Would that be cool?"

"Of course." It wasn't like she needed my permission. It was the Koyamas' house, not mine.

"I don't want to harsh your mellow. I know you probably would like time alone with Zach."

"What? No! I'm fine."

Celeste twirled her hair around and around her finger until the strand was wrapped tightly. Then she let it unravel and started again. She looked nervous. "So, like, it's okay with you? For me to come over again?"

I nodded, a little confused.

"I mean, I'd be hanging out with you. While Noah and Zach do whatever it is they're planning."

"Oh," I said, getting it. "Sure. That would be fun."

I genuinely liked Celeste. It was easy to be around her. And it would be nice to have a friend in Mystic. That had never been a concern before, but now Zach and I weren't friends anymore.

That made me think of Lila. I missed her. I knew our friendship was super solid, but I couldn't help a tiny worry from tightening my throat. I mean, Zach and I had spent a summer apart for the first time ever, and now it felt like we were so different, so changed, that even if I weren't angry with him, I didn't think we could get back to how we were before. I'd hate that to happen to me and Lila.

"Awesome sauce!" Celeste said, bringing me out of my thoughts. She stopped twirling her hair and grinned.

"Let's go, CeCe," Noah called.

"Come on." Celeste leapt off the hammock.

"Where are you going?" I asked.

"*We* are all going downtown."

"Oh, no, you all go ahead. I'm fine." I was not going to go downtown, especially with Zach.

Celeste tugged on my arm. "Please? It won't be fun without you."

Dad waved at me from Holly's car in the driveway. "I'll drive you, Mai."

The guys started piling into the Honda Pilot with Wes.

"Why are we driving?" I asked. It was at most a twenty-minute walk.

"Mr. Koyama is taking all of us back home after," Celeste explained. "Besides, you promised you'd introduce me to your dad."

"Fine."

Celeste hooked her arm in mine and called out to the guys, "I'm riding with Mai!"

When we got in the car, I introduced Celeste to Dad, and she fangirled hard. Dad was nice as always and promised to sign her copies of Teen Time Trekkers. Then he had to go and tell her that the character Amelia was based on me. Celeste got super excited to reread the books with that in mind. I loved that the character was brave and heroic.

On the quick drive downtown, Celeste peppered Dad with a million questions, which was fine by me. I was trying hard to block out the memories of the last time I'd been here.

Dad dropped us off at the usual spot in front of the church to avoid tourist traffic, and said he'd be back in an hour to pick me up. It was hard not to roll my eyes. I was almost thirteen! I should be able to walk back by myself, but I didn't want to argue in front of Celeste.

"Cool beans! This is my first time in Mystic," Celeste said as we walked to Main Street.

Downtown Mystic was only a few blocks long. It used to be my favorite place to hang out until Zach ruined it. Since Celeste had lived so many places, would she turn up her nose at this tiny downtown with shops and restaurants lined up on either side of a narrow two-lane street?

But no, she took it all in stride, as if everything was thrilling. One thing I was learning about Celeste was that she made everything seem like a celebration. She radiated positivity. I really liked that about her.

I made a sharp left at the doughnut shop and led her toward the bridge to the ice cream place where we were meeting the guys.

A sharp toot blasted in the air, and we both jumped. Then I laughed. That dang bridge warning got me every time. "You can always tell the tourists from the locals," I told Celeste. "People who live here never seem startled."

She whooped as the bridge slowly went up, stopping traffic. Even though I'd seen the sight many times, I still loved watching. Tourists were in constant motion, popping in and out of stores, weaving up and down the block, but when that bridge went up, everyone stopped to watch. It was an amazing feeling to be a part of something, even if only for a few minutes.

"You know," I said, "it's not really a drawbridge even though that's what everyone calls it."

"No?"

"It's a bascule bridge. It uses counterweights to raise and lower." I pointed to the concrete blocks lowering toward the street.

"Awesome sauce!"

When the bridge was finally standing straight up like a building, the crowd dispersed, returning to their shopping. We joined the guys in line at the ice cream shop right next to the bridge.

I wasn't sure how I was going to get through the afternoon. But it turned out to be amazingly easy to avoid talking to and even being near Zach. I felt him look my way more than a few times as we ate our cones, then poked around the stores on Main Street. Every time he tried to inch closer to me on the sidewalk or browse with me in a store, I quickly stepped away. Twice I heard him call my name, but I pretended not to hear him. It wasn't hard. All I had to do was ask Celeste a question, and she'd take the long way around to answer.

Yet the closer we got to the bookstore, the more anxious I felt. I loved Bank Square Books. The staff was always nice to me, even though I was a kid. When they'd learned how much I loved birds and nature, they made sure to suggest the best guides and novels each time I came in. I'd save my allowance and gift money to buy a new book or two every summer. But that whale sculpture in front of the store brought back too many memories.

To my relief, the moment we got to the statue, Wes pulled up, and all the boys clambered into the car, including Zach. He and Wes wouldn't be back until tomorrow. I had a reprieve. Celeste hugged me and promised to return next week, then squeezed into the back seat.

I waved to her as the car pulled away, her face smooshed against the glass and her hand waving back wildly, making me smile. But it didn't last. Even though I made a point not to look at the whale and to hurry across the street to Dad's pickup spot, I couldn't stop the memory from rushing back.

Sour

TWO SUMMERS AGO

I stepped out of Bank Square Books clutching my new book to my chest. I had bought *The Sibley Guide to Birds* last summer, but now I had the one specific to Eastern birds. This was one I'd been coveting all summer. Mom and Dad finally caved and gave me my birthday money a week in advance so I could buy it and have time to use it before we flew home for the school year. I was starting middle school and felt a little nervous. We were heading back the day after my party, a week earlier than usual, so I could get all my school supplies together.

I hugged the book, excited to go to the fort and show Zach. He hadn't been home when Dad and I left, but hopefully he'd be there by the time we returned.

I waited in front of the whale statue for Dad. There'd been no parking spots near the bookstore, so he'd dropped me off and would circle around for me.

A sharp toot made me yelp. Cars stopped bumper to bumper as the bridge started to rise. Now it'd be at least fifteen minutes—or longer depending on how many boats needed to pass—before traffic would move again and Dad could make it back.

Hmmm. I could wait in the baking sun or I could dash to the bakery and grab a drink and a cookie. I had change left over from my book purchase. I'd get something for Dad, and if I had enough money, I'd buy Zach his favorite brownie. Though I was supposed to wait right here for Dad to arrive, the bakery was just around the corner. There were a lot of tourists strolling around. I was safe. Mom often told me I was too bold and needed to be more cautious, but Zach called it being brave. I liked that.

Weaving through the crowd, my heart lifted when I saw the back of Zach's head. He was sitting at an outdoor table at Sift, a brownie already in his hand. And he wasn't alone. Ryder and Colt sat across from him, laughing as they tossed flaky bits of a croissant at one another.

That's where Zach was! He'd spent all week with Ryder and Colt. Even though Zach had invited me to join them, I'd refused. I didn't understand why he wanted to waste time with them when our time together was ending soon. Before they'd shown up, this summer with Zach had been the best. I felt closer to him than ever. I wished I could see him during the year, too. Summers weren't enough. I wanted to hang out with him all the time. Luckily those boys were leaving tomorrow, and I'd have Zach to myself again.

I hid behind two men in matching striped shirts, following them until I made it to the bakery. Then I dodged a woman chasing her toddler who clutched a mangled cinnamon bun. He squealed with glee. Fortunately there was a crowd of tourists and I was able to stay out of Zach's sight. I crouched against the low wall surrounding the bakery's wraparound porch just below the spot where Zach and the boys were sitting.

I'd pop out at him. He was going to be so startled. Then I'd convince him to grab a ride home with me and Dad. Smiling to myself, I imagined sitting in our fort together, making plans for my birthday. We would get permission to lay on our moms' hammocks the night before to look for constellations, points of light dotting the dark canvas of sky. It always amazed me how bright the night was here compared to Sunnyvale. Zach called it light pollution—all those street lights dimmed the stars.

"Dude!" Ryder said, interrupting my thoughts. "We should go back to your fort so we can watch that girl dance again."

Maybe I'd been wrong about the boys. They appreciated my dancing at least. I leaned in to hear what else Ryder had to say.

"That was totally hysterical!" he went on. "She was dancing like she was some kind of star."

Hysterical?

"Yeah," Colt said, chiming in. "What was up with that? She looked like she was having a fit."

The boys snorted with laughter.

"And," Ryder said, "what kind of ching-chong music was that? It wasn't even English. Doesn't she like any real music?"

My face burst into flames of anger, and I clenched my hands into fists. I was about to leap out to tell them off, but held back. Zach would stand up for me. He always did. I waited for what would be a totally sick burn.

Instead, Zach laughed. Laughed! I was so dumbfounded I couldn't move.

"Dude! I can't believe you're forced to hang out with her every summer." Ryder again.

I clenched my fists. Come on, Zach . . . say something! He'd always had my back, and I knew now would be no different.

Thirty seconds went by. Then a full minute. Finally Zach cleared his throat. I leaned forward, ready for him to wreck those losers.

"Have you checked out *Road Redemption* for Nintendo Switch?"

That was it?

I pushed my way through the crowd, running back to the whale statue. Why hadn't I waited where I was supposed to? Then again, if I had, I'd have never known that Zach wasn't really my friend after all. I blinked furiously in the sunlight, trying to keep the tears at bay. If I started crying, I would never stop. I didn't want to hang out with Zach anymore. I never wanted to talk to him again. I just wanted to go home to Sunnyvale!

When Dad finally came around to pick me up, I was lightheaded from all the deep breathing I had been doing to calm myself.

"Are you okay?" Dad asked as I buckled in.

I was still breathing heavily. Dad would understand. I mean, while he and the Koyamas got along well, it was really Holly and Mom who were best friends. Dad would be on my side. He would totally be angry when I told him what Zach had done.

"Actually," I started to say, when I hiccupped back a sob.

Dad's eyebrows flew up, and he gripped the steering wheel. "You're not crying, are you, Mai? Are you hurt?"

Dad looked totally panicked. If I started sobbing now, he'd probably fall apart. Tears made him uncomfortable.

"I'm fine," I said, pasting on a weak smile.

Dad released his death grip on the steering wheel. "Well, good. Good. I'm glad."

As he drove us home, I realized that had I said anything, he probably would have told Mom, and then Mom would have pushed me to talk to Zach. That was the last thing I wanted to do.

By the time Zach got home, I had locked myself in my room. I broke the thread around my wrist and flung the stupid rabbit charm he'd given me across the room. I threw it so hard I heard it hit the back wall of the walk-in closet.

I hated Zach. And I would never—ever—forgive him.

6

That evening, I read three books to Ethan and Mason at bedtime, but afterward, instead of joining my parents and Holly on the back porch for a gin rummy tournament, I went to bed. I just didn't feel like pretending to be happy. Only it was way too early for me to go to sleep. It was still light out and I wasn't quite on Eastern time yet, so all I did was toss and turn. Like Dad, I was a night owl.

I got up and peered out the window at the pond. Dusk was just starting to fall, turning the sky lavender. Ducks and geese warbled from the pond. Tomorrow I'd get up early and go birding. I wanted to see the great blue heron that always came to the pond first thing in the morning. Maybe I'd see an osprey, too. For years, I'd wanted to see one catch a fish. I nudged my window open, letting the warm breeze drift into my room.

"Gin!" Mom called from the porch below me as Dad and Holly groaned. Mom was lucky in card games and won often.

I turned to crawl back into bed when a screeching sound froze me in place. It sounded like rusty nails scraping across metal. Goose bumps prickled my skin even though it was warm.

I ran down the stairs onto the porch.

"Did you hear that?" I asked.

"What?" Dad asked.

I put my fingers to my lips, and everyone got quiet. We waited for a few beats and then the screeching started again.

"That!" I said.

Holly nodded. "We heard it earlier this summer and thought someone or something had been injured, but we never found anything. One of the neighbors thinks it's an animal call."

"Cool," I said. "Can I go look for it?"

Dad shook his head. "Holly just said they don't know what it is." He held up his hand at the insulted look on my face. "I know you're not afraid, but I am. Why don't you wait till Zach is here and you can both go?"

Ugh! I was going to go on my own, but I'd wait till the parents weren't watching me. I headed back to bed, determined to solve the mystery. Without Zach.

The next morning, a loud buzzing shook me awake. I blinked in the bright sunlight and bolted upright, banging my head against the ceiling.

"Ow!" The buzzing was coming from my phone. I must have fallen asleep while searching for Connecticut animals that made screeching sounds. It was Lila calling on FaceTime.

"Wow, did I wake you up?" she asked. Her bobbed black hair was neatly brushed, and she looked a little different.

"Are you wearing eyeliner?" I asked.

She grinned and nodded. "Mom finally said I can wear makeup! First official band practice is today."

I rubbed my eyes and smiled. "That's fab! *Everyone* is coming?"

"Yeah, yeah, everyone." Her cheeks turned pink. "I need your opinion."

"On?"

Lila propped her phone up and held up two black tubes of lipstick. "Which one?"

"Let me see them on."

Lila expertly swiped on a dark purple. I nodded. Then she wiped it off and put on a hot pink color.

"That one," I said. "Both look great, but the pink is more you. Good contrast with your hair and eyeliner. Nice wings by the way."

"Thanks," she said. "So, what's the news on the Evil One?"

I flopped back on my bed, holding my phone above me. "Nothing major. We didn't really talk. He brought his friends to the party, so I was able to avoid him."

"Did he seem like he knew you were mad at him?"

I shook my head. "Either he was acting in front of everyone or he was clueless."

"Oh! You should have totally humiliated him in front of his friends! That would have been the ultimate!" Lila spun her drumsticks.

"I thought of that, but I just couldn't come up with anything good. But two of his friends are coming back this weekend."

Lila stopped spinning her drumsticks. "They are? Are they cool?"

"Yeah. Especially Celeste. She's Zach's best friend's girlfriend. She's super nice."

"Oh." Lila looked sad for a brief moment, then seemed to shake it off. "Maybe she can give you some ideas for your revenge. But don't tell her about it! Be stealthy."

"Smart! She's been hanging around Zach since he moved back. She might know stuff that would be helpful."

"Oooh, but wait for me, okay? I want to be there when you finally get your revenge! Plus, best friends have each other's backs. And you barely know that girl."

"I'm not going to tell her anything. It's you and me, Lila, always, but especially for Project Revenge!"

Lila smiled and started spinning her drumsticks again. "Also, you should try to act normal with Zach."

"No way!"

"That way he won't suspect anything. You don't have to be besties but just be friendly enough. It'll make getting him back even better."

Lila was a genius. "True. But I'm no actress. There's no way I can fake my feelings."

"That's totally fine. Just make sure he doesn't know you hate him," Lila said, waving her drumsticks. "Okay, I'd better get ready."

"What's your plan for practice?"

"I think we'll just jam and get a feel for each other's styles."

Lila looked so happy. I wish I could be there, too, even if only as a groupie. "Have fun! And say hiiiiii to Alex for me."

Lila blushed.

"Stay gold," I said.

"Stay gold!" She flashed me a finger heart and ended the call.

I remembered to duck my head as I got out of bed. Once I'd changed into a navy-blue dress and pulled my hair into a high ponytail, I hurried downstairs.

The house was quiet. Dad was either sleeping or working on his graphic novel. I glanced out the window. Neither of the cars were in the driveway, so Wes and Zach weren't back yet. Yay! The twins had to be out with Mom and Holly. They were never this quiet.

I put on my shoes and headed to the fort, humming to myself as I spun the key ring around my finger. When I got to the pond, I stopped to take it all in. I'd missed this place. Waterlilies and cattails grew closer to the banks, but farther out, it was all blue water, quiet except for a few ripples that were probably snapping turtles. Some were the size of raccoons. Those and the muddy bottom kept me and Zach from ever wanting to swim in the pond.

A titmouse scolded me from the branches of the apple trees above, the tufted head feathers looking like a pointed cap. That reminded me of the mystery sound from last night. I'd head out tonight to look for whatever was making it. I wasn't afraid, but I would be cautious. I definitely didn't need Zach's company. More importantly, I didn't *want* it. I didn't even want to see him. Just thinking about him put me in a foul mood.

I stomped the rest of the way to the fort. When I slid my key into the door, it swung open. Had I forgotten to lock it?

My heart nearly stopped as I stepped into the fort. Zach was sitting on his beanbag chair, earbuds in, nodding his head to music I couldn't hear as he flipped through a travel book. I took a careful step backward, hoping to escape before he noticed me, but it was too late. His eyes flew up, our gazes caught, and his face brightened with a grin.

Zach ripped the earbuds from his ears and tossed them onto the floor, along with his phone. So one thing hadn't changed. He was still kind of a slob. Even if he was dressed immaculately in form-fitting black track pants with a white stripe running down the length of his long legs and a white T-shirt with a funky graphic that looked like someone had scribbled on it with a black Sharpie. What happened to the Zach who wore baggy cargo shorts and Mario Bros.–themed socks?

"Amai!" Zach bounded across the room like he was going to hug me again.

I quickly sidestepped and walked over to my bookcase. I crouched, pretending to look for a book.

Zach leaned down next to me. "You okay, Amai?"

"Hmm." I ran my finger across the spines of my books.

He barreled on. "Dad went to pick up his favorite coffee beans. Everyone else drove to grab takeout."

Why was he acting like we were still friends? Why hadn't he gone with everyone else? And why couldn't I muster even the weakest of insults? It was like my brain was stuck. After two years of plotting revenge, I hadn't come up with anything that would hurt him the way he'd hurt me. I was disappointed in myself. I should have dumped his books into the pond when I had the chance. My eyes flicked over to his bookcase. I might still do that, but it wasn't the ultimate humiliation I was going for.

I reminded myself that I needed to act normal around Zach so when Celeste revealed something helpful, Lila and I could make Zach feel bad in a big way. This was going to be a challenge. I swallowed my anger and pulled out *Sibley Birds East*, the very book I had bought the end of that last summer.

"Are we going birdwatching now?" Zach asked.

No, I said in my head. *I'm going birding alone. Without you. Go away!* Out loud I said, "Maybe."

"I have something for you."

I blinked at him, speechless. He hurried over to his trunk, lifted the lid, and grabbed something. Then he swung back around and flung a flat package at me.

Birding had not only made me quick with observations but with reflexes, too. I'd learned to grab my binoculars, point, and focus instantly when noticing movement in the trees. I caught the package with one hand. It was a pink bag dotted with white cherry blossoms.

"In Japan, everything you buy is wrapped like a gift," Zach said. "You would love it. Every time we went shopping, I saw something that reminded me of you. I'm giving you a gift a week until your birthday."

Zach thought of me in Japan? He bought me things? He was giving me gifts all summer? I blinked at the bag in my hand like it might bite me.

A horn honked three times in quick succession, pulling me out of my spiraling thoughts.

"They're back!" Zach leapt up. "Come on! Let's eat!"

He took off out of the fort. Zach was still very food-motivated. Another thing that hadn't changed.

As much as I didn't want to care about the present, I was curious. I ran my finger under the flower sticker that sealed the bag shut, careful not to tear it. I loved stickers and would save this one. And when I tipped the bag, a plastic-wrapped sheet with more stickers slid out, this time of tiny birds. They were adorable. Perfect to use in my birding notebook. My heart wobbled. I didn't want to love them, but I did. Just because they were from Zach didn't mean I had to toss them. I mean, it would be a waste. I'd keep them, but not because I was glad he'd thought of me while he was away.

As I walked back to the house, I reminded myself that I was

angry at Zach with every step. By the time I crossed the driveway, I'd successfully blotted out the weird giddiness brought on
by Zach's stupid gift. The familiar bubble of anger brought me
comfort.

Now I was ready for anything.

7

When I got to the screened porch, everyone was already sitting at the table, including Dad, who looked like he had just woken up. The only empty chair was the one next to Zach. Mom and Holly were distributing plates and silverware while Wes removed take-out boxes from two large paper bags.

"Take a seat, Mai," Holly said. "Wait till you taste the roast chicken!"

"I want to sit next to Mai!" Mason called out.

"No! I want to sit next to her!" Ethan parroted.

I smiled at the twins, my saviors. "If I sit between you, you can both sit next to me."

They cheered.

As everyone shuffled over, our plates were filled with mini tacos, salad, chunks of corn bread, and pieces of roast chicken. My mouth watered. I grabbed my fork and was about to dig in when the twins solemnly said, "Itadakimasu."

"Itadakimasu," Zach, Holly, and Wes responded.

I looked at Mom, raising my eyebrows in a question.

Holly caught my look. "It's what you say in Japan before you eat. It roughly means 'thank you for this food.'"

The twins dug into their tacos, pieces of meat squirting everywhere including onto their laps. I speared a piece of chicken and the juicy, tender meat nearly melted in my mouth. While everyone else chattered away, I kept busy, shoveling food in my mouth so I wouldn't be expected to join in.

"Did you have any favorite places to eat, Zach?" Mom asked.

"Totally," Zach said, putting down his fork with a grin. "This place called Ichiran was my favorite go-to ramen place. But really, I don't think I ever had bad ramen once in Japan."

Holly laughed. "Zach could eat ramen for every meal."

"I tried!" He shrugged. "Anyway, I also loved the street food. Dango, takoyaki, curry-pan. That's Japanese curry inside bread. Amazing!"

Zach picked his fork back up but kept talking. "Mom made curry-pan that came pretty close to the real deal. I used to tag along with her to her cooking classes. Not that I actually took her classes, but it was a great way to hang out and people watch."

Zach finally shut up and got back to eating.

"You're quiet," Wes said to me.

"That's because Zach talks too much," Mason said, defending me.

Everyone laughed. It was true. If Zach liked it there so much, he should have stayed.

Zach passed his plate down to Holly for a second helping of corn bread. When she handed it to me to pass back, I purposely glopped a huge serving of potato salad he hadn't asked for, making sure it touched the corn bread. Then I went back to eating, keeping my head down.

"Mom!" Zach exclaimed, making all the conversation stop. "Potato salad! Everything is contaminated now!"

I held in a grin. "Oops! My bad."

Zach raised his eyebrows at me.

"I forgot you had a thing about mayo." The quick look of confusion that passed over Zach's face was definitely worth it.

Once Zach got a fresh plate with just corn bread, the conversation turned to summer projects. Wes announced, "I promised the twins I'd make them a tree house in the backyard."

"Not too high up," Holly said.

"Right." Wes glanced at me. "Zach's going to help. Who wants to join us?"

I looked at Dad, who had helped build our fort.

He shook his head. "I'll be here on the porch, working. But I'll shout encouragement from time to time."

Wes grinned. "The moms will entertain the twins to keep them safely out of the way."

"I'll do that," I said quickly. I'd much rather watch the boys than have to work with Zach.

"That would be wonderful," Holly said to me. "We can split duties. You can birdwatch in the mornings, and then maybe you can take the twins after lunch for a couple of hours."

I flashed her a double thumbs-up.

The twins cheered. I could see Zach trying to catch my eye, but I stood and started gathering dirty plates. Zach and I alternated days for cleanup, and today was my turn.

"Hold on," Wes said, stopping me. "We have one more birthday gift for Zach."

"Really?" Zach grinned.

We all trooped off the porch, following Wes to the garage. Inside, propped up on sawhorses, was a red canoe.

"No way!" Zach shouted as he circled it. "This is really mine?"

"With restrictions," Holly said.

Zach looked at me. "Amai! We can finally go out on the pond!"

That had been a dream of ours since we were little. I kept my face a neutral mask, hiding the tiny spark of excitement I didn't want to feel.

"Here are the rules," Holly said, raising a finger with each one. "You must go together. No solo canoe trips. You must let an adult know before you head out and when you return. You must always wear your life jackets. No goofing around or standing up or doing tricks. Safety first."

"Got it! Got it!" Zach was nearly skipping around the canoe. "Can we take it out now?"

Ugh. No!

"Yes," Wes said, "because we are going to make sure you both know what you're doing."

Great. I was going to be forced to spend time with Zach.

We hoisted the canoe, which was lighter than I expected, and carried it to the stone steps that led to the pond. When we placed it in the water, it bobbed gently up and down.

"I went canoeing this spring with my friends," Zach said to me.

God. Why did he keep trying to talk to me? Didn't he notice that I wasn't engaging? Was he stupid or stubborn? My money was on stubborn.

We put on matching orange life jackets, but Zach stopped me before I climbed in. "Photo op!"

He held up his phone while our parents looked on wearing huge grins. I sighed and leaned in, careful not to touch him as Zach snapped a selfie.

"One more rule," Wes said. "Leave your phones. That way in case you fall in, you won't ruin them. And instead of documenting every moment, you'll concentrate on being safe." Wes gave Zach a pointed look.

"Look at me!" Mason said. He did some kind of weird walk like he was a model on *Project Runway*. Then he and Ethan fell onto the grass laughing.

"Okay, that's enough," Holly said with a smile. She and Mom took the twins and headed back to the house.

After we both handed our phones to our dads, Zach held the canoe steady as I climbed in the front and held my paddle. Then he took his place behind me.

We pushed off, and I was determined to get this over with as quickly as possible.

"Whoa, Amai," Zach said, laughter in his voice, "you've got some arm muscles on you. But you need to keep the stroke long and smooth. Plus, you're splashing me."

I had a brief thought of tipping the canoe so Zach and his fancy clothes would get soaked, but that would mean I would end up in the muddy pond, too. I adjusted my stroke, and the canoe glided along.

"Good job, Amai. Now alternate paddling on either side so we can stay straight. I want to go over to those birch trees. I'll steer— don't worry about turning."

We got into an easy rhythm. As much as I hated to admit it, canoeing was fun. We made it to the far side of the pond, leaving the house and our dads behind, but still within shouting distance, and stopped paddling.

The cool shade felt good, and I was happy to rest my arms. The front of the canoe gently scraped against the bank, releasing a perfume of mud and wet leaves. I loved the smell of Mystic summers. I tilted my head back, taking in the trees, dressed in papery bark sheaths topped by leafy green hats. Nature's fashion was one I could appreciate. For a long moment, we just floated quietly.

As the canoe bobbed in the water, we rested our paddles across the boat. A pileated woodpecker laugh-called in the distance, but our own silence felt loud.

"How do you like middle school?" Zach asked. "Remember you were so nervous about starting?"

I wrinkled my nose, not turning to look at him. "That was two years ago."

Zach waited a beat, either for more details or for me to ask him a question. Our conversations used to run on forever.

I scanned the trees, spotting a downy woodpecker and a black-capped chickadee. I would go straight to our fort after and add them to my list. I was about to tell Zach I wanted to head back when something caught my eye. I sucked in a breath. I felt the canoe shift as Zach probably followed my gaze up to the sky.

Several high-pitched whistle-chirps in rapid succession came from a bird circling above us. An osprey! Suddenly it swooped and splashed talons-first into the pond. The osprey was so close I could see the dark eye stripes that made it look like it was wearing a mask. I held my breath as the bird flapped in the water. Then slowly the osprey rose with a big fish in its grip! And just like I'd read, the bird shifted the fish so that it was facing forward, making it more aerodynamic for flight.

Zach and I watched in awed silence as it flew off with its lunch.

"Oh my God!" I shouted, turning to Zach. "That was freakin' fantastic!"

"I can't believe we got to see that," Zach said, grinning at me. My heart did a little stutter, seeing his face light up like that. "You've always wanted to see an osprey catch a fish and now you have!"

I nodded, unable to keep the joy off my face. Without discussion, we started paddling back home. I smiled all the way. When we made it to the shore, I leapt out of the canoe and over to Dad and Wes.

"Did you see that?" I asked.

Dad nodded. "You both did great!"

"No! The osprey!" I said.

The dads shook their heads. I couldn't believe they'd missed it. At least I hadn't! I was about to dash off to the fort when Dad said, "Mai, help Zach."

I sighed heavily and trudged over to where Zach was tugging the canoe out of the water, and grasped my end. We carried the canoe back to the garage, my mind focused on recalling as many details about the osprey as possible to write in my notebook. It occurred to me that this very special moment would forever be entwined with Zach and our canoe ride. That was unfortunate, but I was good at adjusting my memory. I could remember the osprey and push Zach aside.

For the rest of the week, I was able to avoid spending any time with Zach. He spent most of the day working on the tree house, while I birded in the mornings and hung out with the twins in the afternoons. Yet whenever I walked through the yard, I couldn't help but get a glimpse of him. Gone were the fancy fashions—he was back in his baggy cargo shorts with the many pockets and ratty T-shirts. On Wednesday as I was walking by, I realized he was wearing his old Nintendo shirt. It was snug and a bit short. He handed a hammer up the ladder to Wes. When he raised his arms, the shirt lifted, revealing a sliver of toned abs.

He spotted me and waved, and my cheeks flushed with heat. He'd caught me staring. Ugh! After that I made a point to leave and return through the screened porch so I wouldn't accidentally run into him.

By Friday afternoon, the twins had their tree house.

"Come see, Mai-nesan," Mason said, grabbing my hand after lunch. Both boys had taken to calling me that. Nesan meant "big sister." I kind of loved it.

I let them lead me to the backyard. They'd been adorable all week, but whew, they had a lot of energy.

Our families gathered at the base of the tree. Holly had been too worried to have Wes and Zach build a proper tree house in the upper branches. Instead, Wes had built a platform about five feet off the ground with the tree trunk running through the center. A ladder led up to the platform, and next to it on raised stilts was a small simple house painted sage green.

The boys scrambled up the ladder like squirrels, barely holding on to the rails. I could see why Holly had been concerned. Those two had no fear. They disappeared into their house and stuck their heads out of matching windows overlooking the yard.

"Papa! Domo arigato!" Ethan shouted his thanks in Japanese.

"Daisuki!" Mason sang his love for the tree house.

Two seconds later, both boys were back down on the ground, racing across the yard toward their bedroom and shouting about all the things they wanted to move into their tree house.

"Well, they are going to have a blast," Dad said.

"What do you think, Amai?" Zach asked me.

"It's nice. They obviously love it."

"Now you and Zach can have a proper summer together," Mom said. "Without the two munchkins in your way."

I clenched my jaw but said nothing.

"Celeste is psyched to see you tomorrow," Zach told me. He had sawdust in his hair and a smear of green paint on his shirt.

"I'm glad she's coming," I said, meaning it. It'd be nice to have someone around that I actually wanted to talk to. Plus, I hoped against hope that somehow she would be able to give me dirt—any info on Zach—that I could use to get him back.

The sooner I got my revenge, the faster I could completely disengage.

8

By the time I woke up the next morning, I was full of good energy. I straightened my room, taking my pile of stuffed rabbits off the other twin bed. Celeste and Noah were spending the night, and I wanted Celeste to be comfortable bunking with me.

I changed into a pale pink cotton dress, slid my phone into the deep pocket, and stepped into the hall. There was a trail of socks and LEGO bricks down the stairs. It looked like the twins had temporarily moved into their parents' room so Noah could share with Zach. I poked my head into the boys' room, and for the first time this summer, their beds were made up, undoubtedly with fresh linens for Noah.

I glanced at Zach's side. Why couldn't I come up with an idea for the perfect revenge? I'd had two years to plan, but all I'd accomplished was stewing in anger while dreaming up ridiculous ideas with Lila. It had definitely felt good, but none of those ideas was doable. Not really. I was now putting all my hope into Celeste.

Frustration pounded at me like pelican wings beating in my stomach. I wanted to do something—anything—to get rid of the queasy feeling. I quickly strode over to his nightstand. His phone was plugged in, so I'd better hurry in case he headed back up for it. I snatched the flashlight and hurried back to my room, hiding it in the bottom drawer of my dresser. Now he wouldn't be able to look for spiders! I hoped he freaked out. Even better if he freaked out in front of Noah. But it wasn't enough, and I stayed irritated.

As I descended the stairs, I scooped up the twins' things and deposited everything in front of Wes and Holly's door.

My timing was impeccable. Celeste came in the back door just as I made it downstairs.

"Mai!" She grabbed me in a hug. "I'm so excited. We are going to have a blast!"

I smiled as I led her back up the stairs to my room. I pointed to her bed, and she looked around, taking everything in.

"You're so lucky," she said. "Not only do you have a room at home, but here, too. You have two spaces to call all your own."

"What's your room like?" I asked.

Celeste sat down on the bed, kicking her bag to the floor. "Smaller than this one for sure, but I like it the best of all the bedrooms I've had. It has a huge walk-in closet with a comfy armchair inside so I can be cozy when I read." She flashed me a smile. "I reread the Teen Time Trekkers books this week. Amelia is still my favorite character. She's brave and loyal and smart. Just like you!"

Okay, well, Dad had told her Amelia was based on me, so even though Celeste couldn't really possibly know those things about me, I did like to believe they were true. It was nice to have Celeste here. I wasn't used to spending so much time alone. *But,* I reminded myself, *being a little lonely is better than being with Zach.*

"The guys are going hiking in a bit," Celeste said. "Do you want to go?"

"Do you?" I asked, being a good host, but silently hoping she didn't.

"Not really."

Excellent! "Let's go hang out in the hammocks," I suggested.

"Zach said you're into birdwatching," Celeste said. "Can you teach me?"

"Sure!" I grabbed the second set of binoculars I had stored in my room, and led Celeste outside.

We lay back in the hammocks, and I handed Celeste her own pair of binoculars, showing her how to adjust them. Then we scanned the treetops.

"There," I said, leaning over to nudge her binoculars to the left.

"Two male goldfinches. They are bright yellow so you can't miss them."

"I see them!" Celeste squealed.

"Oh! Put down your binoculars. Look at the pond." I pointed. "That's a great blue heron. One of my favorites. It's stalking for prey—fish and frogs."

Celeste nodded, a smile on her face. "You sure know a lot about birds. Are you going to be a professional birdwatcher?"

I laughed. "I don't think there is such a thing."

"Sure, like you could have your own TV show or something. *Birding with Mai.*"

We smiled at each other. Who knew? The thought that I could turn my love of birds into a career made me buzz with joy.

"Sorry," I said. "We can talk about other things. What about you? What do you go wild for?"

"Nothing as interesting as birds. But I love playing volleyball. I'm a pretty good setter, and it's a lot of fun. Plus, being on a team helps me fit into whatever new town we move to. Easier to make friends."

I didn't think Celeste needed any help making friends. She was so sweet and open and positive.

"I'm glad you're here," I said, meaning it.

Celeste smiled at me. "I'm glad I'm here, too."

By the time Dad and Wes called us in for lunch, Celeste felt like an actual friend. I didn't laugh when Dad signed her books and she fangirled all over him. And when the guys returned home after their long hike and suggested playing cornhole, I agreed because Celeste wanted to. Making her happy was more important than avoiding Zach.

Celeste and I were so in sync as a team that we won every round. We made up a victory dance that involved jumping jacks and a high five. We laughed ourselves silly while the guys looked on, shaking their heads.

The afternoon flew by, and as we inhaled hot dogs and French fries at dinner—dominating cornhole was hungry work!—I was already feeling sad that she and Noah would be leaving before lunch tomorrow.

After dinner, Wes and Dad got a fire going in the firepit. The twins were super excited because this would be their first time making their own s'mores. They were bouncier than ever, and I questioned the wisdom of giving them sugar so close to their bedtime.

"We bought special s'mores marshmallows," Mom said, holding up a bag of gigantic marshmallows.

"Thanks, Sumi," Zach said to my mom, catching the bag. "Sugoi!"

Holly looked at me, "That's Zach's overused phrase for 'awesome.'"

"Hey." He fake-scowled. "I haven't used it much since we got back to the States!"

I helped Mason while Zach assisted Ethan on my other side. Stabbing a marshmallow onto a stick, I guided it closer to the fire. "Not in the flames," I instructed. "Better to roast them over the hot coals."

"Okay, Mai-nesan!"

But the extra-large marshmallows were heavy, and Mason's quickly drooped off the stick and fell into the pit.

Zach tried to compensate by turning his stick constantly, but Ethan got annoyed. "I can do it myself!" he cried, yanking the stick out of Zach's hand. Two seconds later, the marshmallow fell into the fire.

"I've got an idea," I announced, threading two sticks into a new marshmallow to give it more stability. That seemed to work. Everyone else did the same.

When I finally helped Mason construct his first s'more, my heart soared with triumph. I definitely showed up Zach, who was still struggling. He'd now dropped three marshmallows into the fire. I ticked a checkmark in the column of my imaginary scoresheet of *Mai versus Zach, Who's Better?* I gloated. But then I looked up to see Celeste with gooey marshmallow everywhere. On her face and hands, and in her hair. These treats were T-R-O-U-B-L-E!

I quickly turned to snatch the s'more from Mason, but it was too late. He took a big bite and the melted marshmallow oozed out from between the graham crackers all over his hands. Undeterred, Mason chewed heartily as more marshmallow dripped from his hands and onto his shirt. Ugh!

"Zach! Get Ethan!" I shouted quickly.

Zach lunged for Ethan as I grabbed the sticks from his hands. We fell into an easy rhythm, tag-teaming our efforts to corral the twins. But as I pulled the sticks toward me, Ethan snagged the marshmallow. With his hands.

"That's hot," I shouted. Zach scooped the marshmallow from Ethan before he got burned. Melted marshmallow stretched in a long thread from Ethan to Zach.

"Gross!" Zach groaned as Ethan tried to lick the marshmallow off his hands and only succeeded in smearing it all over his hair and face.

"Maybe these marshmallows weren't such a great idea," Mom said, laughing.

By some miracle, I hadn't gotten any on me. I turned to Celeste. "You want to go back in the house and clean up? Then we can hang out in my room before bed."

Her eyes brightened. "Awesome sauce!"

I glanced at Dad. He'd fallen asleep with his marshmallow in the fire, burning it to a crisp. I pulled the stick out of his hand and tossed the entire thing into the pit.

"Poor Ty," Mom said. "He's loving drawing his graphic novels, but this deadline has been keeping him very busy."

I kissed Dad's forehead, glad I'd skipped making s'mores myself, and led Celeste back to the house. Once she'd cleaned up, we changed into our pj's and climbed onto our respective beds.

"Tonight was totally awesome," Celeste said. "Thanks for letting me share your room."

"I'm glad you're here. It was fun." I smiled as I slid under my covers. Wes had installed the window AC units on Friday, and now it was comfortably chill in my room. In just a couple more weeks, Lila would be here. And that reminded me of her advice. Time to see if Celeste had any intel I could use.

"So, you've been hanging around Zach a lot, right?" I asked.

"Yeah, pretty much. Noah and I got together in October, and then Zach came back in March."

"What's the funniest thing you've seen Zach do? Anything embarrassing?" I asked.

"Hmm. No, not really. He's pretty quiet."

Zach was quiet? "Is he still terrified of spiders?"

"Zach used to be afraid of spiders?" Celeste asked.

"He's not anymore?"

She shook her head. "A few weeks ago while a bunch of us were hanging out in Noah's basement, Zach went through all this trouble of catching a spider and taking it outside to set it free."

"Really?" That was not the Zach I remembered. Stealing his flashlight today would not affect him after all. At least he had rescued the spider. That was an improvement.

"Yeah. For a while, the guys were all calling him Spider Boy."

Could I use that? No, that wasn't juicy enough. "Anything else you can tell me about Zach?"

Celeste sat up and grinned at me. "I get it."

"What?"

"You and Zach."

Ugh. She was getting the wrong idea. I waved my hand. "It's not like that."

"Don't feel weird about all his followers," she said.

"His what?"

"You know, on Instagram."

"Zach has an Instagram account?"

"Uh, yeah." She giggled, her eyes wide with disbelief. "You didn't know?"

"I'm not allowed on social media until high school," I said. "And the last time I saw Zach was two years ago. He wasn't allowed to have an account then, either."

"Ohmigod!" Celeste squealed. She leapt off her bed, grabbed her phone, and bounced onto my bed, almost hitting her head. "You have got to see this!"

I sat up as Celeste tapped on her screen and then handed the phone to me. My eyes nearly bugged out of my head. "*This* is Zach's account?"

"It is!" she said with unbridled glee.

I read his bio out loud. "Zach Koyama, Tokyo teen model now based in Connecticut. Loves to travel." He had close to five thousand followers. I looked at Celeste. "He was a model in Japan?"

"I can't believe he hasn't told you any of this." Celeste smiled. "He did some modeling as a favor to a friend at his international school, and it turned into a regular gig for him. He's saved all the money he made so he can take a gap year to travel before college."

I blinked. Who was this guy?

I scrolled through his posts. Every single photo of Zach looked like a fashion shoot. His clothes were definitely model-worthy, and each pic could have been straight out of a magazine. I hated to admit it, but he looked cute.

I noticed one name popping up over and over in the comments. "Who's bisou_bisset?"

"Oh, don't worry about her! Marietta Bisset was a girl at his school in Tokyo. Apparently she was after Zach, but he isn't interested. I asked him, and he doesn't have a girlfriend right now."

I felt my face get warm. "I don't care about that."

"Anyway," Celeste said. "We tease Zach because he takes his account so seriously. The rest of us post goofy things. Zach only posts his very best pics. He calls it his professional account."

"He wants to be a professional model?" It was more and more apparent to me that I no longer knew Zach the way I used to. This made it easier to let go. I didn't know this Zach at all.

Celeste shook her head. "I don't think so. But he has followers from all over the world, so he's all about keeping up his image. Noah's always threatening to post embarrassing pics of him just to wind Zach up." Celeste caught my look. "But he'd never actually do it!"

Maybe Noah wouldn't, but I would! I grinned as I handed Celeste her phone. She went back to her bed and climbed under the covers.

"Hey, Mai?" she said quietly. "Today was fun. Thank you."

"No, thank *you!*" I finally knew how to get my revenge, thanks to her.

"Mai?"

"Hmm?"

"Can we be friends? I mean, I would never try to replace Lila or anything, but it would be totally awesome to have a girl friend."

I smiled sleepily. "Sure. We are definitely friends."

"And I promise to be all those things you said a friend is. Loyal. Honest. I'll always be on your side, Mai."

My eyes snapped open. She sounded so sincere. But all I could think about was how her words echoed another promise I'd gotten long ago. Despite the chill from the air conditioner, sweat prickled my skin as the memory came rushing back.

SEVEN SUMMERS AGO

It was a hot day. Beads of sweat rolled down my back and tickled my skin. Zach and I were waiting for our dads at the whale statue in front of the bookstore while Mom sat on a low wall, reading, not far from us. I hugged the picture book she'd bought me about a family of owls. I'd picked it up because of the pictures, but when she explained it was written in haiku, a type of Japanese poetry, I made her read the book to me. Twice. I couldn't wait to get back to the house. Maybe Zach would read it to me again later. I could read okay, but Zach was seven and much better at it.

As usual, Zach and I played hidden pictures at the whale while we waited. There were lots of little paintings on the statue.

"Find a guy rowing a boat," I said.

I waited while he circled the whale until he called, "Found it." Then I checked to make sure it was the right one.

"Find an origami boat," Zach said.

He stayed put while I searched the whale, walking around and examining it closely. I was so intent on finding the picture that I walked into a boy a little bigger than me.

"Watch it," he growled.

"Sorry," I said, glancing at my mom. She was on the phone talking to someone.

"Why don't you look where you're going?" he said, standing much too close to me. I tried to step back, but the whale was behind me.

"Hey!" Zach came around the whale. "Don't talk to her like that!"

The boy's eyes got big, and he scurried away to his family, who was renting bikes in front of the store.

Zach patted my shoulder. "Are you okay, Amai?"

I nodded. "Thank you. He was scary."

"I will always look out for you," he said, his hands on his hips like a superhero. "That's what best friends do."

"We're best friends?"

"Of course!"

"What does that mean?" I asked. I had never had a best friend before.

"It means we're friends forever. We have fun together, go on adventures. We look out for each other. Protect each other. I'm on your side, Amai, always."

Zach took my hand and walked me over to my mom, who'd spotted the dads and was gathering up her shopping bags so we could head back to the house.

Zach and I were best friends. I felt warm and safe, and like he promised me, I would always protect him, too.

9

Two days after Celeste and Noah left, I finally caught up with Lila on FaceTime. She was busy with band practice and a volunteer job, and that plus the time difference made it hard to catch each other.

"So?" I asked. "Tell me everything about the Hot Pinx!"

Lila spun her drumsticks. "It's so great! Everyone is meshing. I can't believe how well we all play together. And Iris's voice is amazing."

"Wow. That's great, Lila!" I was so happy for her. She'd been wanting to put together a band all year, and now it was happening! "What songs are you playing?"

Lila nodded. "So far, just some covers by the Chocolate Flamingos. Turns out we all love their music."

That was an alternative rock band Lila really liked. "Cool," I said.

"Right? And maybe if that goes well, I'll share one of my originals."

"Wow, really?" Lila composed music, too. She was *that* talented, but she'd never shared them with anyone except me. Not that I could properly judge or offer anything helpful other than saying everything she did was great, because it was.

"I think between all of us we could come up with some great arrangements. Turns out Quinn writes poetry, so maybe she can write lyrics, too!"

For some reason, I wanted to change the subject. It wasn't that I was jealous or anything, but this all felt so weird and different. Usually I'd be right there experiencing everything with Lila. I mean, if I had stayed in Sunnyvale, it's not like I'd be in the band, but I *would* be there as their audience of one at least. Maybe even choreographing dance moves.

"Hey," I said, "how's Alex?"

Lila's cheeks flushed pink.

"Oooh," I teased. "Tell me!"

"There's nothing to tell. It's just nice seeing him every day, you know? We're getting to know each other better, but . . ." Lila stopped.

"But?"

"He seems to talk with me more than anyone else in the band."

She dropped her eyes, smiling. Then she looked back up at me, embarrassed. "Not that I'm obsessively keeping track or anything."

"Of course not. Maybe you can invite him to stay after practice one day. To work on a song. A loooooooooove song," I teased her.

Lila waved her hand at me, but her smile said she liked my teasing.

"Enough about me," she said, still grinning. "What's going on with you?"

"I think I have an idea for the perfect revenge," I said.

"Mai!" Lila squealed. "This is huge! Why didn't you lead with that?"

I caught her up on how Zach had an Instagram account full of modeling pics and how we could post embarrassing ones.

"That's genius!" she said. "Okay, first you need to get the passcode for his phone."

"I know," I said. "I'll find out what it is before you get here."

"And you're going to have to get some cringeworthy shots of him. Maybe as he's coming out of the bathroom with dripping wet hair or something."

"Gross! I'm not waiting around while he's using the bathroom. Besides, there are tons of photo albums around the house. I can take pics of the truly humiliating ones and load them to his account."

"You are brilliant! I can't wait!" Lila said, smiling. She waved her drumsticks at me. "Wait, how did you find out about his Instagram account? Did he tell you?"

I shook my head. "Celeste! Remember? I told you I would get her to spill."

"Excellent! You've been texting with her?"

"Actually, she slept over a few nights ago."

"She did?" Lila's drumsticks went still.

"I can't wait till you're here," I said. "I miss you."

Lila put her drumsticks down, out of sight. "I miss you, too."

"Just another week and a half, and we'll be together," I said. That made her smile.

"Mai!" Mom called.

"I have to go," I said. "Mom and Holly are leaving on their annual NYC trip."

"One day that will be us!" Lila said.

"Truth." I held up my pinkie to the screen. "Stay gold."

She touched hers to the screen. "Stay gold."

Downstairs, I joined the families in the driveway. Dad was going to drive Mom and Holly to the New London train station.

Mom gave me a hug. "You'll be okay?"

"Of course. This isn't new," I said. She and Holly took a special BFF trip every summer for a couple of nights.

"But this year you and Zach have to help out more with the twins," Mom reminded me.

"No big," I said. With Dad on deadline, he'd be home but needed to work as much as possible. Wes wouldn't be around much because he had meetings in Fairfield.

Holly turned to the boys. "Remember, you promised to behave and listen to Zach and Mai."

"We promise," Ethan answered for both of them.

I wasn't too worried. The twins had a ton of energy and could be mischievous, but they were never naughty. The worst part of all this was having to share babysitting responsibilities with Zach.

"Thanks, again," Holly said, smiling at me and Zach. "After this, you two are free to do whatever you want for the rest of the summer."

We waved as the car drove off.

"Tree house!" Mason yelled. The two boys tore off toward the backyard.

"Are you ready for this?" Zach asked.

"As ready as I'll ever be." I was prepared to be the best actress in the world. Plus, being nice to Zach might help me get his passcode.

We sat in the backyard while the boys played in their tree house, making a racket.

Zach waved his Switch at me. "You want to play Mario Kart?"

I shook my head and instead scanned the trees with my binoculars.

I counted three goldfinches (two females and one male), five bluebirds, and a house finch. I especially loved bluebirds and cardinals because I only saw them here. It was mostly mourning doves and crows in Sunnyvale. Off in the distance, in between Ethan's and Mason's squeals of joy, I heard a Carolina wren singing its teakettle song. These birds, their songs, these moments all added to the specialness of Mystic.

Zach groaned as his game ended, bringing me back to reality. I cleared my head. All those good feelings were in the past.

"Mai-nesan!" Mason shouted. "Ethan took my rock!"

"I did not!"

I sighed, pushed myself out of my chair, and walked over to the platform. "Okay, guys, that's enough. Come on down."

"See what you did?" Ethan said. "Tattletale!"

"I am not!"

I could tell from the wobble in Mason's voice that he was about to cry. That would lead to a meltdown that would be hard to recover from.

"Oh, boys! Look who just pulled up in the driveway," I called. "Dad said he'd take us to get a treat. The big question is, would you rather argue or go get ice cream?"

"Ice cream!" Mason and Ethan chorused, back on the same team again. They quickly scurried down the ladder, nearly knocking me over in their haste to get to Dad, who had just walked into the yard.

"We're hungry!" Ethan sang.

Dad smiled. "Let's go, then."

After we'd gotten our cones and taken a long walk to help burn off the twins' unflagging energy, we picked up an early dinner from Nana's Bakery & Pizza. Throughout the day, I didn't really talk to Zach, but I didn't avoid him, either. I needed him to think all was well.

Back home on the porch, Dad ate a salad while sketching in his notebook. Like some dads might look odd without their glasses or a trademark hat, Dad would not look like Dad without his sketchbook or tablet.

I leaned over him as he finished drawing what looked like Godzilla climbing the Mystic Bridge. "Ha," I said. "Good one."

He smiled at me.

"How's the book going, Ty?" Zach asked as he wiped pizza sauce off the boys' faces.

"Pretty good. I mean, it's getting down to the wire, but I'm feeling confident I'll meet the deadline." Dad gave me a look. "Sorry about this."

"It's fine, Dad."

"Yeah, Ty, we understand. I can't wait to read the next book," Zach said. He gave up on Mason, who ran back into the house with cheese in his hair. Ethan sat still for Zach because he worshipped his big brother.

"Poor Zachy," Ethan said, looking up with wide eyes. "All work and no play."

I laughed only because Ethan looked so forlorn at the thought of his hero not getting time to goof off. That would seem horrible to Ethan for sure. Playing was his life. I remembered what that was like when Zach and I were Ethan's age.

Dad set his notebook down on the table with a smack. "You're right, Ethan. Zach and Mai have been working hard." He smiled at me. "You two can have the evening off. I'll get the twins to bed."

I pressed my lips together. I didn't really want to spend time with Zach, but I'd been waiting for a chance to investigate the strange sound at night. I'd heard it again the evening before. And it looked like Zach had, too.

"Oh yeah!" Zach said. "Amai, we can figure out what's making that noise!"

"Great! It's settled," Dad said. "But let me know when you get back. Don't stay out too late after dark, and keep your phones on. No going off the property."

So. Many. Rules! "Okay, Holly," I said.

Zach laughed.

"Very funny," Dad said, smiling. "You two can go now, if you'd like."

"Thanks, Ty," Zach said. He turned to me. "Meet you back here in twenty."

I grabbed the dirty dishes and stuck them in the dishwasher. After I tossed everything else in the trash and recycling bins, I changed into jeans and long socks. The mosquitos were brutal. I also grabbed my tote bag and tossed in my mini first-aid kit, some baggies in case we found anything cool, latex gloves in case we found anything gross, and bug spray. I also snagged the camping lantern, checking it to make sure the batteries didn't need replacing.

Zach was waiting for me at the back gate in baggy cargo shorts and a ratty green long-sleeve T-shirt. It looked like he either got dressed without looking or hadn't done laundry because he wore one red and one blue sock with old hiking boots. A neon-yellow baseball cap perched on his head. He couldn't wear more clashing colors at once if he tried. Maybe I could get a pic of him wearing all that and post it.

"You ready?" he asked.

"Yep." I was walking a high wire, balancing my anger at him with trying to be friendly enough that he wouldn't suspect an ambush.

"Which way?" he asked.

"I think I heard the noise coming from behind the fort." I led the way past the garage. Wes usually cleared the brush back here, but it looked like he hadn't had time yet. I was glad the trail was too narrow for us to walk side by side. We walked in silence, listening for the mysterious sound, but we still hadn't heard it by the time we reached a small clearing on the Koyama property line where Zach and I used to come to watch the stars. Behind their property was a huge field belonging to the neighbor. We took our usual seats on two stumps—mine slightly taller, and Zach's with a little bit of a back to it. I called it his throne.

"At least it's not that humid," Zach said, peering at me.

I averted my eyes and leaned back to stare up at the night sky. Just two summers ago, we'd sat here, looking up at the stars sprayed out across the night sky.

"See that?" he'd said, pointing. "Those three stars are Orion's belt."

The warmth that had spread through me as Zach taught me the constellations had nothing to do with the summer heat and everything to do with Zach.

Crickets and cicadas chirped and buzzed tonight just as they had two years ago, but nothing felt the same. It used to be easy, hanging out with Zach, talking about anything and everything. But I wasn't comfortable anymore. I was just about to suggest heading back when we heard it.

A high-pitched screech that made my skin prickle and raised the little hairs on the back of my neck.

"Sugoi!" Zach said in an awed whisper.

"Sugoi," I said, trying the word out.

Zach smiled at me.

"We need to figure out what that is," I said quietly. "Could you tell what direction it came from?"

Zach shook his head. "It sounded like it came from everywhere. Like we were surrounded."

He seemed a little freaked out, and that made me smile, not in meanness, but because it was familiar.

"If we hear it again, we need to try to figure out where it's coming from." We'd promised Dad not to stay out late, and I knew he wouldn't want us wandering aimlessly. Or at all.

We sat there for another half hour, waiting for the sound and watching the stars.

This time, the silence felt like home.

10

I woke up early the next morning, changed into my floral-print dress, and slipped quietly down the stairs. Everyone was still asleep, making it the perfect time for me to go through the photo albums. I pulled them out from a nook next to the fireplace and sat on the couch.

I didn't bother with the pictures of Zach as a toddler. No matter what he was doing in the photo, it would be adorable. Instead, I started with the album of the summer he turned ten. Maybe I could find a shot of him picking his nose or after a bad haircut. I flipped through the pages quickly, not wanting anyone to come downstairs and see what I was doing. Luckily I found plenty of photos with Zach in clashing colors and bad fashion.

I stopped on a page. He looked ridiculous. He'd turned some jeans into shorts with a pair of scissors but hadn't bothered to measure, ending up with one pant leg above the knee and the other below. He wore a pink Kirby tee under Holly's green-and-orange Hawaiian shirt. I'd forgotten how that summer we used to play fashion show, taking old clothes and trying to improve on them. Except Zach's outfits were always disasters. I couldn't stop the laughter from bubbling up. That had been fun. I squinted at the succession of photos, each outfit of Zach's worse than the one before.

This was striking as close to gold as I could have hoped for. I snapped pictures with my phone.

When I got to the album from two summers ago, our last one together, I hesitated, not sure I was ready to let these photos take me back there. But they were the key to my revenge, so I opened the album on my lap. The first spread showed his birthday party, the one he'd hoped to trade with me. We were both wearing obnoxious party hats. His was a goofy bucket cap made to look like a birthday cake with candles. In one photo, he was making a seriously hideous face. I grinned as I shot a pic of it.

I turned the page, and there we were, arms draped over each other's shoulders. On my wrist, the rabbit charm Zach had given me hung from a blue thread. In another picture, Zach and I shared a plate that held a giant slice of birthday cake, our heads close together, laughing at some joke. You had to hand it to Mom; she was really good at taking pictures, especially candids. My heart wobbled. There

Zach and I were, before he ruined us. There was the way we looked at each other, our matching smiles, the easy way we sat together, almost always touching.

Slamming the book shut, I shoved the albums back into the cubby. My face burned as I took off to the fort. The first thing I did was get my notebook, but when I lifted the lid of the bench, a gift bag sat on top of my books.

I stared down at the bag as a confusing tangle of emotions knotted in my stomach. The Zach who had come back from Japan seemed so different. Not only in the way he dressed but overall. He looked older and acted more mature and calm. While I still hated him, it was hard to mesh the Zach I once adored with this new version.

Opening the bag, I peered inside and pulled out a flat rectangle wrapped in light blue silk with a gold floral pattern. It was the same kind of good luck amulet that relatives in Japan had sent us when I was little. I looked in the bag again and spotted a note in Zach's familiar printing.

Amai—
I got this shiawase omamori at a Tokyo shrine. It's for happiness. I hope you're always happy.
—Zach

I dangled the charm from my finger. He hoped I was happy? Was that his way of apologizing? I shook my head. *Not good enough, Zach.* I wouldn't forgive him that easily. But that didn't mean I couldn't keep his gift. I'd hang it off my school backpack.

I spent an hour birding. After adding over twenty species to my bird list, including my first sighting of a red-bellied woodpecker, I packed up, feeling calmer and more myself. Instead of heading back to the house, I turned left onto the trail and made my way back to the stumps. Now that it was light out, I could return to the clearing without checking in with Dad. I wouldn't be able to investigate the mystery sound, but I could look for treasures. When I was in fourth grade, a wildlife biologist came to our class. She said she was nature's detective, scouting clues to glean information. Scat, or animal poop, revealed a lot—it could tell you what kind of animals were in the area and what they were eating. Most of my classmates were completely grossed out, but I'd been fascinated. Living in a city, I thought we didn't have wildlife, but I'd learned we had plenty in our backyards—squirrels, ducks, raccoons, possums. It was like discovering a whole world I hadn't known existed.

Back in the clearing, I saw some deer scat and some tracks, but nothing else. Well, just the faint footprints Zach and I had left behind the previous night. It had been a pleasant evening. My stomach fluttered.

Just as I was about to head back to the house, something on the ground caught my eye. When I kneeled to get a better look, my heart raced with recognition. An owl pellet! I scoured the ground and found another dried-out one. I gently tucked them in my pocket. Score! More treasures to add to my nature collection.

I was still grinning when Zach met up with me in the driveway.

"Why so happy?" he asked.

"I found something super cool!" There was no way I could hold back when I was this excited. Plus, I needed to be nice. I had embarrassing photos, but without his passcode, they were worthless.

"What?"

I pivoted to head back to our fort, Zach close on my heels. Inside, I sat down at our table and Zach took a seat across from me. Then I dropped both pellets in front of him.

Zach shoved his chair away. "What are those?"

I took a small amount of joy that he was still as squeamish as ever. "Owl pellets!"

"Like poop? Amai! That's disgusting!"

I laughed wholeheartedly for the first time since arriving in Mystic. "No, not poop. More like barf."

"Arghhh! That's worse!" Zach stood up and backed away.

I grinned. "How is that worse?"

He scrubbed his face with his hands, looking like the Zach I remembered. "I don't know! It just is."

I grabbed a piece of paper from my notebook and put the two pellets on it. Then I started to tear a pellet apart with my fingers.

"What are you doing?" Zach said, sounding horrified.

I laughed again. "Come sit and look. Owls eat their prey whole. Everything they can't digest forms a pellet, and they regurgitate it up."

"And why do I want to see?"

"We can figure out what the owl is eating by identifying the bones we find. Probably mice. This gray stuff is probably the fur."

Zach made gagging sounds.

"Oh my God, Zach. Stop! Just sit down. I won't make you touch anything."

He inched back to the table and sat as I separated the pellet fluff from bones.

"Do me a favor and look up a rodent bone chart so we can identify these," I told Zach, pointing to a small skull and a bunch of tiny bones.

Zach dutifully took out his phone and started searching. I wiped my hand on my dress and held it out. But Zach scrunched his nose. "You are not touching my phone with your owl puke hands."

"They're clean!"

"Not!" Zach held up his screen to show me a chart of rodent bones.

"I can't see. I need to zoom." I reached for the phone, but he yanked it away. Huffing with impatience, I said, "Fine. Print it up, and I'll grab the chart from the house later." Then I smiled. Wishing I could force Zach to hand me his phone gave me an idea.

I worked on the second pellet while Zach looked on. At least he'd stopped making gagging sounds. Now he actually looked curious.

"Those two skulls don't look the same," he noted.

"I think these are legs, maybe?" I pointed to a small pile of similar-looking bones. "Let's go back to the house and get the chart from the printer."

We walked across the driveway to join Dad and the twins for lunch, and I hummed a happy tune. I couldn't find it in me to be snappish or rude. I was in too good a mood. The twins laughed as Zach and I took turns telling silly jokes, giving Dad a bit of a break.

After lunch, I made sure that Zach saw me wash my hands thoroughly. Dad was taking the twins on a hike, so we headed back to the fort—we had bones to identify—and I purposely left my phone behind.

The printed chart helped us figure out we had a mouse skull and maybe a shrew. The tinier skull was broken, so we couldn't be sure. Now that Zach had latex gloves, he was fine with handling the pellet contents. The thin bones were ribs, not legs as I had thought.

"Hey," I said as casually as I could. "I forgot my phone. Can I use yours to take a few pics? My hands are clean." I took off my gloves and waggled my fingers at him.

"Fine." He peeled one glove off and slid his phone across the table to me. Then he went back to sorting bones.

"What's your passcode?" I asked.

"Seven-one-one-eight-one-three."

I was surprised. Those were our birthdates. And easy for me to remember. I snapped photos of the bones, and when he wasn't looking, I took a few of him. His hair wasn't styled, and he was wearing a ratty old Mario Bros. T-shirt that had moth holes in the shoulder. Definitely not his usual fashion-perfect outfit. I made sure to get a shot of him picking through the bones, too. More embarrassing pics to post!

"Can I text these to myself?"

"Go for it." Zach didn't even look up.

I quickly texted all the photos and then deleted the text and the incriminating photos from his phone. I was proud of my spy skills and smiled to myself as I put his phone back on the table.

"Hey, Amai, everything okay?"

"Yeah, why?"

"Just checking in with you."

I reminded myself I needed to stay cool because the second part of the plan meant I had to get ahold of his phone without him around in order to post all the embarrassing pics I'd collected.

"Talk to me, Amai. Remember we promised to always share our feelings."

As if! That was then. This is now. I wasn't sharing anything with Zach anymore.

"I'm fine." I brushed my hands off and scooped up the bones, snatching them from under Zach's nose.

"Hey!" Zach frowned.

Ignoring him, I arranged the bones on my bookshelf and without another word, I was out the door. I didn't want to remember making that promise to each other.

But like I said, sometimes memories had a life of their own.

FOUR SUMMERS AGO

"Zach," I whined. "Please talk to me."

He raised the *Super Mario Adventures* comic book in front of his face and kept ignoring me.

I sat on my side of the fort, wondering why he wouldn't answer. Was it because I played with Ethan and Mason all morning? That didn't seem fair. They were his brothers, and at two years old, they were finally fun to play with. I flipped back through my memory, looking for the exact moment when Zach had stopped talking to me. It was at dinner last night that I'd first noticed his silence. So it probably didn't have anything to do with me playing with the twins this morning.

"Zach?"

He flipped a page angrily. I couldn't remember a time he'd been so mad at me. Ever since Zach had turned ten this summer, the slightest thing could set him off. I sat on my bench pretending to look through my binoculars, but I couldn't focus on anything except the pounding of my heart. I blinked back tears, refusing to cry or to let Zach know how much he was hurting me.

I heard him shift behind me, and in the reflection of the window, I watched him toss the comic book onto the floor. He looked my way, and my heart leapt. Maybe now he would finally tell me what was wrong. Maybe he would give me a chance to apologize for whatever it was.

But no. He got up and left without a word.

That was it! I couldn't take it anymore! I ran out after him and found him sitting on the stone steps leading to the pond's edge, past the apple trees. I took a deep breath and joined him, sitting close enough that he would know I was there but not so close that he'd bolt.

"I'm sorry," I said quietly. "Tell me what I did so I can fix it."

A tiny ant marched past my feet, using its antennae to feel its way across the stone. Pat, pat, step, step, pat, pat, step, step. I watched as if it were the most fascinating thing I'd ever seen. When it finally reached the grass on the other side, I blinked back tears and swiped my hand across my eyes.

Zach sighed loudly. "That's not fair," he said.

He talked to me! "What's not fair?" I asked.

"You're crying. You know I feel bad for you when you cry," he said softly.

"I'm not doing it on purpose." I rubbed my eyes, but the tears kept coming.

Zach scooted closer to me and put an arm around my shoulder. I was so relieved that the dam burst and I started to sob, leaning my face into his shoulder. But soon I was all cried out. "Tell me what I did," I said with a loud hiccup.

He sighed again. "You didn't stand up for me when Mom was nagging me about watching the twins."

"When?"

"Yesterday morning! Mom said she'd asked me to watch Ethan and Mason, but she hadn't! You were right there with me the whole morning. You could have told her that she hadn't said anything. And then this morning you watched them without being asked, so you made me look even worse! Best friends stand up for each other!" His face turned red in anger.

"I'm sorry, Zach. I really am. I didn't mean to make you look bad."

He dropped his arm and shrugged. I knew he didn't like it when his parents were upset with him, especially since the twins had come along. He wanted to be the perfect son, the perfect brother.

Holly and Wes were totally mellow, so I didn't get why he felt that way. It wasn't like they expected perfection.

"I'm very sorry for not saying anything to Holly. Just tell me when you're mad, okay? I can't fix things if I don't know what I've done wrong. Zach, I don't like fighting with you."

"I don't like fighting, either," Zach said. "Let's promise to always tell each other how we feel."

I scrunched my nose.

"Come on, Amai," Zach said, nudging me. "Feelings aren't horrible."

"Ha-ha."

"I'm sorry, too," Zach said. "Next time I'm upset, I'll tell you. Okay?"

"Okay."

I made that promise even though it wasn't easy for me to share my feelings. But there was nothing worse than having Zach angry with me. I hated wondering. I hated not knowing. And so I'd promise Zach the world if it meant he wouldn't keep secrets from me. But even as I made that promise, I wondered if it was a good idea.

When my alarm went off the next morning, I groaned. Ethan and Mason had been totally wound up last night, partly from missing Holly. I'd put them to bed at their usual time, but then they woke up almost every hour on the hour until well past midnight wanting glasses of water, escorted trips to the bathroom, or just hugs. Zach and Dad had slept through all of it, of course.

I climbed out of bed and reminded myself that Mom and Holly were coming home today. I'd be done chasing the twins around the house and the yard.

After I got dressed, I ducked my head into the boys' room. Zach was still sleeping. He lay curled up on his side, the blankets pulled almost all the way up over his face. I could see his hair, sticking up like porcupine quills, and his eyes fluttering as if watching a dream. What did he dream about? Walking a catwalk for Fashion Week?

Adoring, screaming girls lunging at him? He mumbled something and flipped onto his back, flinging an arm over his face.

I quickly turned to the twins, but their beds were empty. That was not a good sign. Hurrying down the stairs, I hoped I wouldn't find any massive destruction. So I was relieved to see Dad on the couch with his sketch pad and Ethan and Mason nestled on either side.

"An elephant wearing booties," Mason said. Both boys leaned over Dad's sketch pad, making me wonder how Dad could see what he was drawing.

The boys applauded. Then Ethan said, "A spaceship underwater!"

I came up behind them and peered over Dad's shoulder, watching him draw super fast. This was a game he'd played with me and Zach when we were younger.

Dad leaned back and smiled at me. "Your turn?"

"To watch the boys, yes. Not to draw." Dad's talent had not trickled down to me. "Thanks for watching them."

"No worries." Dad stood, tucking his sketchbook under his arm. "We already ate breakfast. I'm going to do some work before I leave to pick up the moms."

I smiled.

"Remember, they're bringing home Zabar's for a late lunch," Dad said as he disappeared back upstairs.

"You guys want to play in your tree house?" I asked the twins. It was still early enough to do some good birding.

"Yes!" they shouted.

I grabbed an everything bagel and a glass of juice, then snagged my notebook and followed the boys into the backyard. They disappeared into their tree house, but I could hear them trading Pokémon cards.

After I'd left the fort abruptly yesterday, I'd avoided being alone with Zach. I wasn't unfriendly, because I still had a part to play, but I also didn't want Zach to pry. I had to be careful not to get too comfortable. Stay on his good side. It was a little exhausting, and I'd be happy once Lila got here to help me get my revenge. She and I were partners in everything, unlike me and Zach. I could count on her help just like she could always count on me.

My phone buzzed with a text. There was no way Lila was awake yet. I smiled when I saw it was Celeste. We'd traded numbers when she was here last, but I hadn't heard from her at all till now.

Celeste Williams
Good morning!
Is this too early for you?

Mai
Nope. I have twin duty.

Celeste Williams

I tried to do some birdwatching but I need you!
All the birds look the same.

Mai

It will get easier with practice.
Next time you're here we can go birding again.

Celeste Williams

I can come back?

Mai

Of course!

Celeste Williams

Awesome!
I'll talk to Noah & see when we can visit again.

Unknown number

Dudes! Give a guy a break. I was sleeping!

Celeste Williams

HA! Wake up Noah! Or should I call you Sleeping Beauty?

I hadn't realized we were on a group text. I checked the list, and sure enough Zach was on it, too. I added Noah to my contact list.

Zach Koyama

Noah would sleep all day if he could.

Noah Murdocca

Z! You're supposed to be on my side.

Zach Koyama
I'm on the side of truth!

The screen door slammed, and Zach walked out into the yard, freshly showered, wearing jeans and an unbuttoned blue linen shirt over a snug rust-colored tank top. He looked like a bluebird.

Zach moved a chair next to me and sat. He peeled a banana while I sipped from my mug. I tried to think of something to say to make things between us feel normal. When had I ever had to work so hard around him? Oh yeah, since he'd ruined everything.

Dad came outside and called, "I have to run a few errands before heading to the train station. Who wants to come?"

"Me! Me!" Mason shouted.

"Me too!" Ethan said, racing down the ladder. I gripped my mug tightly, as if that would keep him from falling. Yeesh. No wonder Holly hadn't wanted a real tree house for those two.

Dad gathered the twins and took off.

"Everything okay?" Zach asked.

"Yep."

"You were kind of, I don't know, maybe shy or something when you first got here."

"Shy?" I rolled my eyes. "Why would I ever be shy around *you*?"

"You're just quieter than usual."

"Whatever," I said.

"Okay, so it's the other thing, then."

I turned to look at him. "What other thing?"

"I totally get it. You know, your mood swings," Zach said.

My what? "Excuse me?"

"I get it," Zach repeated.

"What do you get?"

"I've been hanging out with Celeste, so I've gotten used to the monthly mood swings. Kind of."

I narrowed my eyes at Zach. "What exactly are you trying to say?"

"You know." He squirmed.

"No. I don't."

Zach's cheeks turned pink. "Hormones. Girl stuff."

Despite the heat on my face, anger won over embarrassment. "Are you blaming my mood on my period?"

Zach's face flushed a deeper red. "I'm just saying you don't have to feel bad about it."

"I don't feel bad! And, also, I didn't have my period when I first got here. But even if I did, it's none of your business. Don't ever blame a girl's mood on her period. It's like saying her feelings aren't real because hormones are taking over."

Zach ducked his head. "Okay, sorry. Point taken."

"Don't ever joke about that," I said, getting in the last word.

Silence grew between us as I took a few deep breaths to calm myself.

"Thanks for calling me out," Zach said.

I cocked my head at him. Was he being sarcastic? As I searched his face, I could tell he was being sincere.

"Here's to honesty." Zach raised his cup of juice. "I like it when we can talk about things."

Whatever. I looked up in the trees, scanning for birds.

"Nuthatch," Zach said, pointing to the redbud tree.

"Got it, thanks." I added it to the list on my lap.

"What's that one over there?"

I followed Zach's finger and saw the brief flit of wings as a bird took off. "I think that was a black-capped chickadee."

We spent the rest of the morning in the backyard together, keeping conversation strictly to the birds we spotted or heard. But I couldn't help thinking about Zach's comment about honesty. He was so far from honest he couldn't find it with a map.

Or maybe he'd just never been honest about us being best friends in the first place. Sure, we'd been close when we were kids. But maybe by two summers ago, it was no longer true. I thought we'd had the best summer ever, but maybe it had meant nothing to him. Maybe I meant nothing to him. I shook my head to clear it of all the maybes. There were just too many.

Before I knew it, I heard the car pull up.

"Mason! Ethan! Those hands need washing before we eat!" I heard Holly call.

"The moms are home," Zach said with a smile. "No more Twin Tornado cleanup! Now we can just hang out for the rest of the summer like we used to. Just the two of us."

But that was exactly it. I didn't *want* things to be the way they used to be. Not if it meant having a friendship I could never trust. I stood up and took a deep breath. I just had to hang in there for one more week and a day. When Lila arrived, we'd get my revenge. And then I'd never have to talk to Zach again. But until then, I had to keep pretending.

We joined everyone on the porch for a delicious Zabar's lunch. Mom and Holly had had a blast and spent the entire lunch regaling us with everything they'd done, seen, and eaten while in New York. I made sure to hang around Mom the rest of the day, acting like I'd missed her, which I had. It was an easy way to avoid Zach.

And I kept it up all evening, and into Friday morning. Wes had returned, and both families decided to head to the beach on Saturday. Dad left his tablet at home, and Mom and Holly brought along the leftovers from Zabar's for lunch. I swam while Zach made sand sculptures. Later when I was drying off on my towel, baking in the sun, I listened to the waves rolling in as Dad and Wes played catch with the twins.

After lunch, I walked along the shore looking for rocks and jingle shells.

"Hey," Zach said, falling into step next to me.

"Hey." The boiling anger I'd felt yesterday had lowered to a simmer. It was hard to stay full-on angry when everyone around me was acting so light and happy. And Dad was finally taking a weekend off. He and I had played Frisbee for an hour before lunch.

"Here, I found this." Zach handed me a piece of cobalt-blue beach glass the size of a quarter.

"It's gorgeous," I said, holding it up to the sun. I handed it back to him, but he shook his head.

"It's for you."

Why was he always giving me presents? Did he think he could bribe me into forgetting that he'd betrayed me? I held the glass out to him. "That's okay. You found it; you keep it."

"I don't want it. I found it for you. You're the one who collects rocks and shells and stuff."

I curled my fingers around the smooth glass and tried to spot the flicker of false friendship in his brown eyes, but instead he gazed at me warmly with a quirk of his lips. It was the kind of smile that meant he felt like all was right with the world.

I couldn't help but mirror his smile. It seemed like the most natural and easy thing to smile when he smiled. Because the truth was, I was happy. Both of our families were here at the beach like previous summers. Mom and Holly were laughing and making jokes. Wes and the twins played catch. And Dad built an amazing sand sculpture of Charmander and Squirtle, Ethan and Mason's favorite Pokémon characters.

"It's nice to see you smile, Amai," Zach said. "This is what summer is about, right? Our traditions."

And just like that Zach vaporized all the joy. Traditions! Those were for friends. We were not friends. Not anymore. Not after he'd betrayed me. Not after he was okay with those boys' racist statements. Not after he'd lied about always having my back.

I reminded myself that I only had one more week till Lila arrived. I could do this, keep fooling Zach into thinking all was well.

I tucked the beach glass into my already-bulging pockets. We ended up walking for an hour, gathering more treasures: a sand dollar, an empty hermit crab shell, one perfect gull feather.

When we got home that evening, I arranged everything I'd collected on my bookcase in our fort, and studied the beach glass Zach had given me. My shoulders raised and lowered in a heavy sigh. Curling my fingers around the glass, I squeezed it, recalling his smile as he'd handed it to me that afternoon.

If I was being honest, reminding myself over and over how angry I was at Zach was exhausting. The more I pretended I was okay with Zach, the more it started to feel real. I wasn't even sure if I was acting anymore.

I placed the dark blue beach glass front and center on top of my bookcase.

When we returned to the beach on Sunday, I wanted to just relax and enjoy myself. To forget, at least until Lila arrived to help me, that I hated Zach. I'd done the work, and I was sure Zach didn't suspect a thing. I deserved a break. So after lunch, Zach and I took the twins in the water. They'd been begging to play water tag, and I didn't have the heart to keep saying no. Plus, their giddiness was catching. My ears rang for hours after, listening to them squeal as they dove away from whoever was "it." At one point, Zach laughed so hard, he ended up with a mouthful of ocean and snorted it out of his nose. Then I ended up swallowing salt water when my mouth was open laughing at him.

I hadn't expected it, but I was actually sad to pack up our stuff and head home. Because after thirty-four rocks, sixteen jingle shells, five sandcastles, three meltdowns (two for Mason, one for Ethan), and one piece of cobalt-blue beach glass, it finally felt like summer to me.

12

When I woke up on Monday, I felt light inside, as if a heavy burden had been lifted. Smiling, I got dressed, bouncing on my toes like music was playing. I promised myself that I'd go back to hating Zach when Lila arrived in four days. Not that I'd ever really stopped hating him. I hadn't. Zach was still the enemy for sure. But after the weekend at the beach, laughing and having fun with the families, I was committed to my earlier decision of just letting go and relaxing.

I nearly skipped to the fort. Zach was already there, leaning back in his beanbag chair, eyes closed, earbuds in. I softly stepped over to him and yanked out the earbuds, startling him.

"Amai!" Zach grabbed his chest like I'd given him a heart attack.

I laughed.

He grinned. "Maybe now I won't give you your next gift from Japan."

I pretended nonchalance and shrugged, walking away and dropping into my chair at the table. My ears were on high alert, though, and I smiled when I heard him opening his trunk.

Zach took his sweet time rummaging around in the chest. I pretended to not care, but I was bursting with impatience. Finally he tossed a package at me. I caught it, using my lightning-quick reflexes.

Zach watched as I peeled back the pretty handmade white wrapping paper that was shot through with threads of gold. This was a keeper.

"Ha! I knew you'd save the paper," Zach said with a grin.

It was my turn to grin when the paper fell away. Inside was a notebook with a gorgeous bird on the cover. The bird had metallic-green breast feathers that joined with inky-black plumage at the belly. The back, wings, and tail were a light gray color. The most striking thing about the creature was its head—dark blue neck feathers and a bright red face.

"What kind of bird is this?" I breathed in awe.

"It's a green pheasant, the national bird of Japan."

"It's amazing!"

"Right? The minute I saw this notebook I thought of you."

"Where did you get it?"

"At the international school I went to. One of the teachers is a painter and sells her work."

I ran my finger over the artwork. I would save this notebook for something very special. And I wasn't leaving it behind when the summer ended. It was coming home with me for sure. "What was the international school like, anyway?" I asked.

"Just like any other school, except fancier, with students from all over the world."

"That must have been different from your totally white school in Fairfield."

"Hey. It's not totally white. Just mostly. The international school was pretty awesome. And we had a lot of choices for classes and activities."

"Like?"

"I took a music appreciation course that got me into Japanese rock. And a Japanese language intensive."

"I hear you speaking Japanese with your family. That must be nice." I was a little envious. I only knew a handful of phrases. "You must have really liked living there."

"It was incredible! And the sights were awesome—the temples, Mount Fuji, the museums, and Tokyo itself. Whatever I do in the future, it will have to involve travel or living abroad."

"You're thinking about your future?" Zach had never been a planner.

He pointed to the books on his shelf. "These are all the places I want to go to first. But I keep buying more books, so who knows where I'll start. I'm collecting travel guides like you collect bird books."

My head spun. Even though I'd been angry for the past two years, I'd always assumed he and I would see each other regularly. If he traveled or moved out of the country again, he'd just be . . . gone. That made my chest tighten in a way that surprised and annoyed me. I didn't want to talk about this anymore.

"Any guesses on what's making that scary sound at night?" I asked.

"I was thinking about that. I searched online. Maybe it's a fisher cat."

"What's that?" If it wasn't a bird, Connecticut wildlife wasn't my strength.

Zach took out his phone, and I moved to sit next to him. He scrolled to a picture of what looked like a cute little weasel. I leaned forward to get a better look, and I could feel his breath, warm, on the back of my head.

"It's so cute!" I exclaimed.

He tapped a button, and a horrible screaming came from his speakers.

I jerked back, my head grazing his chin. "That awful sound is coming from that adorable creature?"

"According to this site, they're pretty vicious killers."

"Well, that's disturbing." I shook off the shivers. "But it doesn't really sound right. The fisher cat sounds like a kid screaming. The other sound is more, I don't know, unearthly."

"Both sounds are creepy."

"Aww, are you scared, Zachy?" I teased.

"No!" He said it so quickly and defensively that we both laughed. "Well, I will admit that the sound is a little scary, but it's not like it's a ghost or anything."

"Can you be sure of that?" I raised my eyebrows and made a scared face.

He grabbed my arm and squeezed gently. "Don't do that! You know I'm not as brave as you are!"

I smiled, and then he did. But Zach didn't release my arm. His hand felt warm.

"Okay," I said. "Let's sit out on the porch every evening. If we hear the sound, we'll go exploring."

"Deal," he said, finally letting go. "You want to take the canoe out?"

"Sure. Why not?" Maybe we'd see another osprey.

Zach stood and headed for the door. And for the first time in two years, I didn't think about anything but following along.

13

Mai
You there?

Celeste
Here!

Noah
Here!

Zach
I'm here but Mai knows that cuz I'm sitting next to her.

Mai
Har har.
Can you two come to Mystic on Monday?

Celeste
Sure!

Zach

Dad and I will pick you two up and bring you back.

Noah

Cool! What's going on?

Mai

My BFF is visiting for a few days from CA.
I want you all to meet her!

Celeste

AWESOME! Can't wait!

I couldn't, either! The rest of the week flew by, and I was finally having fun. Now that we didn't have to watch the Twin Tornados, Zach and I fell into our old summer routine of spending time at our fort, watching movies with the family (while Dad usually fell asleep), exploring around the pond, and researching the mystery sound, even though we'd stopped hearing it.

On Friday, I woke up super early and cleaned my room. I couldn't wait to see Lila! But I still had hours until we picked her up at the airport, so I headed to the fort to kill some time.

First, I turned on the wireless speakers and started with "Stay Gold" by BTS, humming along to the music. Then I reorganized my nature collection and straightened my bird books. As my BTS playlist continued, I felt like dancing but held off. I'd dance with Lila when

146

she got here. I smiled just thinking about it. We hadn't had a chance to video chat lately. And texts just weren't the same as actually hanging out.

"Amai! Come quick!"

Zach's voice sounded panicked. I dropped everything and bolted out of the fort. Heart pounding, I ran toward his voice and saw him chasing a cat through the apple trees.

"What's going on?" I panted as I caught up to him.

He spun around and headed back toward our fort. "I saw that cat pounce on a bird. I scared the cat away, but I'm not sure if the bird is hurt."

"Oh no!"

We ran to the lilac bush. I was terrified we'd find a lifeless body. But just as we reached the bush, a robin burst into flight through the branches.

"Was that it?" I asked, watching the robin disappear over our fort.

"I think so."

We squatted and examined the ground. No bird, injured or dead. No blood. No loose feathers. We stood up, and I turned to Zach, grabbing his shoulders with a smile. "You chased off the cat before he could do any damage."

"I'm relieved!"

I dropped my arms and moved even closer to Zach. I was so proud of him for rescuing the robin. "I wish people would keep their cats indoors, or at least put bells on their collars. Did you know that domestic cats kill over two billion birds a year in the US alone?"

"Wow. That's a lot of birds."

"You saved one, Zach. You're a hero!" My smile stretched so widely that my cheeks hurt.

"There you are, Mai-nesan!" Mason ran over to us. "We're leaving for day camp now. Will you come with us?"

"To camp?"

"No, silly! To drop us off!" Mason shuffled his feet side to side. He was nervous. The boys had never gone to camp before and didn't really want to, but Holly definitely wanted the twins to expend some energy elsewhere. She'd signed them up for three different single-day camps, and this was their first one.

"Aw, I wanted to go with you," I said, frowning like I was super sad. "Hiking and learning about plants sounds fun. And maybe you'll see some turtles."

Mason's face lit up. "I like turtles! Let's go!"

I looked at Zach. "No doubt Ethan will want you to come along, too."

"No doubt." Zach grinned.

We all piled into the car with Mom and Holly. The drive to the Mystic Nature Center and Camp took all of ten minutes. As soon as the car was parked, Mason and Ethan tumbled out and ran to the building, Mom and Holly chasing after them. Zach and I were slower to get out of the car.

"Well, I have no idea why they wanted us to come," I said, laughing. "They forgot all about us!"

As we walked toward the building, a sign caught my attention.

"Hey," I called over to Zach. "Check this out. They have rescue animals here."

"Really?" Zach rested his elbow on my shoulder as he read the sign.

"Let's go look." I grabbed his arm and tugged him along a narrow path that went past the office building and down a hill. We approached a bunch of large enclosures made of wood and wire with signs identifying each animal and the reason it was there.

"This squirrel fell from a power line," Zach said.

"Aw, poor guy." I read the sign. "Oops. I mean, poor girl. But it looks like she's fully recovered and will be released back in the wild soon."

Zach and I walked down the path, bumping shoulders as we checked out the rest of the animals.

"You excited about your friend visiting?" Zach asked.

"So excited! I only wish she could stay longer than four days."

"Why can't she?"

"Her parents. She has a volunteer job that she promised she would take seriously." That was part of the deal she struck with them in order to have a band and practice all summer.

When we approached the last enclosure, I gasped. A gorgeous owl stared back at me. Its white face was framed with tiny tan feathers in an almost heart shape. It had a snowy-white chest and tan feathers on the rest of its body. I'd never seen one for real before, but I knew what it was.

"A barn owl," I said in awe.

Zach read the sign. "Hit by a car and broke a wing. It had to be amputated. Oh, that's so sad. But it looks like she will stay here to educate people about owls."

Just then, she let out a horrible screech and swayed from side to side, her one good wing raised at us. Prickles ran down my back, and Zach grabbed my hand. We looked at each other, wide-eyed, recognizing the sound.

"Don't worry about Dolly," a voice said behind us. An older woman with a gray ponytail joined us. "She's just telling you not to get too close. I'm Margie, the director of the center."

"That sound she made," I said, dropping Zach's hand. "Is that how all barn owls sound?"

"Pretty spooky, isn't it?" Margie said.

"I think there might be a barn owl living near us," Zach said. "We've heard that exact sound in the evenings this summer."

Margie raised her eyebrows. "Really? That would be fantastic. The barn owl population is declining in Connecticut because of reduced habitat."

"I found owl pellets behind the garage a couple of weeks ago," I said.

"Are there any open spaces nearby?" Margie asked. "Barn owls prefer hunting in fields and grasslands."

Zach shook his head. "Only small clearings. We're next to Egret Pond."

"Oh, yes," Margie said. "That means you're by the Philbricks' farm. They actually have a pretty big field on their property. One a barn owl might be attracted to."

Mom and Holly joined us, having dropped off the twins. I introduced them and told them what Margie said.

"Would it be possible for me to come check out the site?" Margie asked. "It would be great to confirm if we had a barn owl in the area."

I was giddy. If Margie found the owl, maybe she'd show it to me. I hadn't checked off any owls on my birding list yet.

"Come by anytime," Holly said. "I'm glad we know what that sound is now."

This was the best day of the summer yet! Lila was arriving, Zach and I had solved the mystery, and there was a chance I might get to see an owl! I was in such a good mood I suggested we stop and get ice cream downtown on the way home.

Zach and I goofed off on the drive there, changing the lyrics to songs on the radio so every one was about owls.

"Owl be there for you," I sang.

"I only have owl eyes for you," Zach sang later.

"Hooting to the beat, y'all," I warbled.

"Good gracious," Holly said, laughing. "You two are almost worse than the twins!"

We found an actual parking spot on Main Street, which never happened. More good luck. After we ate our ice cream, Mom and Holly walked arm in arm ahead of us. Zach and I did the same, following them down the block, our arms hooked together feeling natural and right.

"I need to pick up a book for Dad," Mom said. "Let's stop by the bookstore, and then we need to get ready to pick up Lila."

I must have had a huge grin on my face because Zach laughed. "You look goofy happy."

"I am!"

Mom and Holly went into the bookstore, but Zach and I decided to wait outside by the whale statue. It was a gorgeous day, and nothing could ruin my mood. Everything was, as Celeste would say, awesome sauce!

"Remember that game we used to play when we were kids?" Zach asked.

"Yeah. Hidden pictures or whatever we called it." I turned to smile at him, but he was gone. Whatever. I started a list of all the places I couldn't wait to take Lila. A record store I knew she would love, the cute gift shop with awesome stickers, and the bakery, for sure.

Suddenly hands grabbed my shoulders from behind, and I squealed. I spun around and came face-to-face with Zach.

"Gotcha!" he said, laughing.

"Ha-ha. That was not very nice!" I scrunched my nose at him, the same way I used to when we were younger. His hands lingered on my shoulders, and I remembered when he'd saved me from that mean boy when I was little, right here by the whale. Zach used to make me feel so safe. A joyful warmth spread throughout my body like liquid sunshine. I squinted up at him, a smile on my lips.

Everything around us seemed to freeze. I heard only the pounding of my heart as the sounds of cars and the crowds faded away.

The sidewalk, the storefront, the whale all disappeared from my view. It was as if I were in a tunnel and Zach's face was at the end of it, inching closer and closer to me. Our eyes locked, and I moved toward him like we were magnets. Zach paused, inches from my face, and I closed my eyes, tilting my head up to him.

Then Zach's lips were on mine. His kiss was soft and gentle, and I automatically kissed him back. His hands tightened on my shoulders, and I leaned toward him.

Suddenly reality slammed into me. What was I doing? Zach *used* to make me feel safe, but now I wasn't sure how to feel about him. I gasped and pulled away, stepping back and nearly tripping over a dog behind me. Confusion swirled inside me, twisting and turning my stomach.

"You two ready to go?" Holly asked as she and Mom stepped out of the store.

I didn't answer but pivoted and nearly ran back to the car, relieved that Mom and I would be leaving immediately for the airport.

As I stared out the window on the drive home, the river came into view. Holly was taking the long, circular scenic route back as she often did. I craned my neck to look for the nesting pair of ospreys on a platform, reminding me of the time Zach had surprised me by inviting me on a bike ride and taking me there. So many good and happy moments with Zach created each summer, wrecked by one memory.

And now that kiss. It had triggered a flood of happy memories. And it made me feel like I wanted to spend all my time with Zach. But how could that be? I hated him. Right?

Sweet

SEVEN SUMMERS AGO

"Close your eyes and put out your hand," Zach said.

I did as he said. Then something small and feather light tickled my palm.

"Open your eyes."

In the center of my hand was a tiny ring made from a single blade of grass. I lifted it to my face. "Did you make this?"

"Yes! It's for good luck when you go back to school," he said. I was starting first grade in the fall.

"It's cute," I said.

"Here." Zach took it back and then slid it onto my ring finger, tightening the loop. Then he chortled. "Ha! Now you have to marry me!"

"What?" I cringed. "Nooooo!"

"Yes! If you wear my ring on that finger, it means you have to marry me!"

Our parents laughed in the way they did when they thought one of us was being cute.

"I'm taking it off," I said, reaching for the ring.

"It doesn't matter. You already put it on. It's like a promise, and you have to marry me." Zach danced around the room.

I looked at my parents, my eyes filling with tears. Mom tugged me over to her and gave me a hug. "Why so sad?" she asked. "That just means Zach loves you. Don't you love Zach?"

I nodded into her shoulder.

She whispered in my ear. "It's just a nice gift. You don't have to marry him if you don't want to."

I peeked over Mom's shoulder. Zach had settled down to make another ring from a pile of grass in front of him. Was he making one for someone else? I didn't like that at all! I pulled away from Mom and ran over to Zach. I put my hand over the small pile of grass. "You don't have to make any more. I'll keep this one."

Zach grinned up at me. "And marry me?"

The truth was Zach made me happy. I wanted to spend every summer with him for the rest of my life, like Holly and Mom. I glanced at both sets of parents, grinning at us like we were the sweetest things ever. Mom had married Dad. Holly had married Wes. They got to spend all their time together. That was even better than only summers.

I blew out a breath. "Yes, fine. I'll marry you."

14

"Mai!"

I startled out of that long-ago memory to see Mom knocking on the passenger side window. We were parked at TF Green Airport. Pushing open the door, I stepped out into the late-afternoon sun.

"Are you okay?" Mom asked, shaking her head. "You've been awfully quiet."

I fell into step next to Mom and hunched my shoulders. "Sorry."

We crossed the small parking lot to the terminal. "I bet you're just excited to see Lila. You were daydreaming the entire drive here."

I blew out a breath in an attempt to shake off the memory of Zach's "proposal." It had come up unbidden while thinking about that kiss. Or while trying *not* to think about the kiss. I reached up to touch my lips but quickly dropped my hand. I should be angry.

Why had Zach kissed me? I tried not to think about how I'd stupidly kissed him back. All the play-acting and pretending we were friends again had gone to my head and made me think it was real. Made me forget the sweet boy I'd spent the morning with was just an act, too. Zach didn't care about me. Not really. So I needed to refocus. I needed to be angry!

But not now. Now I got to be happy because my real best friend was almost here. I shoved the memories and the weird, confusing feelings deep down where they belonged.

"I can't wait to see Lila!" I shouted. I nearly dragged Mom through the process of getting us to the gate. Mom had to meet with the flight attendant and sign a release form since Lila was twelve and traveling alone.

"Yep, you're excited," Mom said, a little out of breath.

People started to exit from the jet bridge, which meant Lila's flight had landed. I waited, bouncing up and down on my toes, until I recognized her trademark silver Puma high-tops. She wore them all the time.

"There she is!" I squealed. I ran to the doorway just as Lila stepped through and yanked her to the side so she didn't block the people behind her. We jumped up and down, screaming and laughing and hugging.

"You're here!" I shouted.

"I'm here!" Lila's grin matched mine.

"Hello, Lila," Mom said, joining us. "Welcome."

"Thanks, Mrs. Hirano! My mom told me at least ten times to be sure to thank you."

We laughed on our way to the luggage carousel.

On the drive back to the house, I interrogated Lila for all the latest news. "Tell me everything! The Hot Pinx must be getting really good. You brought videos, right?"

"Two!"

"Two!" I pumped my fist in the air.

Mom took the earlier exit so Lila could see the river view.

"It's so pretty in Mystic," Lila said. "No wonder you love it here."

Used to, I corrected in my head. *I used to love it here.*

"It's very peaceful," Mom said, agreeing. "We really missed coming here last summer."

Not me.

We drove onto the Koyamas' property, which I'd described in great detail to Lila, but she still looked at it with wide eyes. "A pond! You have your very own pond!"

No. Zach has his very own pond. This isn't my place. Not anymore.

Mom caught my eyes in the rearview mirror, and I realized I was being weirdly quiet.

"We can go exploring tomorrow," I said.

When Mom stopped in the driveway, a heavy sense of dread weighed on me. How was I supposed to face Zach? He'd kissed me and confused me about everything again! I couldn't just act like nothing had happened, but I seriously didn't want to talk to him about it, either. I just wanted to hate Zach Koyama! I really, really did!

"Where's the Pilot?" I asked, realizing the other car wasn't here.

"The Koyamas went out to dinner to give Lila a chance to settle in and let the two of you have some time together. You know how excited the twins can get with new people."

I was relieved. I wouldn't have to see Zach just yet.

I gave Lila a quick tour of the house and herded her up the stairs to my room. Then I closed the door behind us.

"It's huge!" she said.

"Right?" I grinned.

Lila sat on her bed across from me. "First things first, how are we doing on Mission Instagram Hack?"

I would finally get closure. "All set. I have his phone passcode and a folder of embarrassing pics of him ready to AirDrop. We just need to separate him from his phone so I can upload them."

"How are we going to do that?"

"I figured it out. You ask Zach to take you out on his canoe. He'll have to leave his phone behind—our parents' rule. While you two are on the pond, I'll grab his phone."

Lila nodded. "Brilliant!"

I gave her a solemn look. "Will you be able to fake being friendly for the sake of the plan?"

She grimaced. "I'll take one for the team. It will all be worth it in the end."

I leaned forward with a pinkie out, and when she hooked hers around mine, we both said, "Stay gold!"

Oh, how I'd missed her! "Okay," I said, changing to a happier topic. "The videos!"

I crossed the room to sit next to her, and she cued up the first video on her phone. The opening to their cover of "Truly Madly Pink" by the Chocolate Flamingos burst from the speakers. I knew the band would be good, but I was blown away. They were outstanding! Lila's drumming was spot-on—she looked like a real rock star. Iris's vocals were fierce, and Quinn and Alex sang backup while playing their guitars like they were born to do it.

"Lila, the Hot Pinx is Billboard ready! Wow!"

She laughed. I could tell by the flush of her cheeks that she was pleased. Next she showed me the second video, a ballad.

"Seriously, Lila. You all are amazing!" I sighed, feeling a little left out. I wished I had been able to stay home in Sunnyvale this summer. Fangirling at their rehearsals would have been a lot more fun than stressing about Zach.

"Thanks! I'm not sure we're ready to play in front of people. You and Tomás, who recorded the videos, are the only ones who have heard us. But maybe by the time school starts, we can think about entering the talent show."

"Who's Tomás?"

"Alex's cousin."

"How is Alex anyway?"

Lila fiddled with her phone and then plugged it in, placing it on the nightstand between our beds.

"Lila? Is everything okay?" Alex was a nice guy, but he had better not have upset her. I would tell him off for sure! Nobody hurt my best friend's feelings and got away with it!

"Well . . ." She trailed off.

"What?"

She covered her face with both hands and then said, "He kissed me."

"What?"

Lila spread her fingers and peered out at me, her grin spreading across her face. I grabbed her hands, and we both squealed.

"Lila! Tell me everything!"

She giggled. "Alex started staying after band practice to help me clean up. He only lives two blocks away, so he doesn't need to catch a ride with Iris and Quinn. Last week, after we finished putting all our gear away, I invited him in for a snack."

"Brilliant," I said, nudging her. "Go on!"

"We were sitting on the couch, talking about music, and then he asked me."

"What do you mean he asked you? Like if he could kiss you?"

Lila flushed a deep red and nodded.

"That's adorable," I said. What would I have said if Zach had asked first? I mean, of course I would have said no! What was wrong with me? Why was I thinking about stupid Zach? "And how was it? The kiss?"

"Perfect." Lila swooned and fell backward on her bed, staring up dreamily at the ceiling. "What was *your* kiss like?"

"What?" I spluttered. How could she know that Zach had kissed me?

Lila sat back up, giving me a look. "Gideon Yoshimura?"

"Oh, that!" I said with a sigh of relief.

"You forgot about your first kiss?"

"That didn't count," I said. "I didn't even like him." It was at a party for Lila's orchestra class that she'd invited me to at the end of the school year. During a game of truth or dare, Gideon had chosen dare. We were the only two Japanese Americans playing, so when he was told to kiss someone, everyone shouted it *had* to be me. Because I was Asian, too. Like that was a thing. We had both been embarrassed, and Gideon had apologized right before he gave me a quick peck on the lips. I hadn't even kissed him back. It wasn't exactly the most romantic kiss ever. My thoughts flashed to my kiss with Zach, and I scowled. That had felt romantic, but I definitely didn't want to count it as a first kiss, either. Not when I didn't understand why he'd done it. Or why I'd gone along with it.

"When did this happen?" I asked, wanting to keep the focus on Lila.

"Four days ago! I wanted to tell you immediately, of course, but since I was coming here, I figured it would be better in person." She couldn't stop smiling.

And neither could I. "Are you two together now?"

Her phone buzzed with a text. She checked it and giggled. "It's Alex. And yes, we're together."

We fell back on the bed, squealing again. As she texted him back, her smile grew even bigger, if that was possible.

I knew I should tell Lila about my kiss. I never kept secrets from her. But I didn't really know how I felt about it. I wanted to be angry. I mean, I *was* angry! But I was also confused. And if I couldn't act with the right amount of indignation, Lila, who knew me better than anyone, would see right through it and get the wrong idea. She'd think that maybe, just maybe, I was happy that Zach had kissed me. And if she thought that, she wouldn't go through with our plan. Lila, while loyal, was also softhearted. She wouldn't be on board with humiliating Zach if she thought there was even the slightest bit of hesitation on my part. And I needed to get him back. I really needed it. I would tell her about the kiss . . . after our plan succeeded. And maybe by then I'd know how I really felt.

I looked over at Lila, texting with her new boyfriend. I was very happy for her. Her dream had come true, and soon she would help make mine come true, too.

After dinner, Mom and Dad took the leftovers to the kitchen while Lila and I chatted about what we'd do the next day. When the Pilot pulled into the driveway, my chest tightened. I took a deep, calming breath.

"Here we go," I said to Lila. "Are you ready?"

She straightened her shoulders and nodded. "Operation Revenge is on! Watch me be super nice to your mortal enemy all for the sake of our plan. You can call me Secret Agent Pinx."

The twins leapt out of the car and ran screaming over to us. I'd warned Lila about their boundless energy. The screen door banged open as they charged onto the porch and threw themselves at me.

"We missed you, Mai-nesan," Mason said.

"I missed you, too! This is my friend Lila."

"Hi, Lila!" they chorused. Then they shouted, "Tree house!" and ran out into the backyard while Holly tried to corral them for bath time. Good luck with that.

Lila and I turned back toward the driveway. There stood Zach looking like a model in mirrored aviator glasses, faded black jeans, and a pale pink linen shirt, the sleeves rolled to his elbows. My traitorous heart stuttered. *But only because his outfit kind of, sort of reminds me of Jin from BTS,* I told myself. He smiled and started to come our way.

Lila's breath hitched. "Holy drumsticks, Mai, you didn't tell me he was so pretty!"

I glanced at my best friend. "It's only the clothes."

Lila raised her eyebrows. She was about to say something but held it in as Zach stepped onto the porch. I made quick introductions, and Lila managed a strangled "Hi." The parents joined us, and Wes deposited a box containing a plethora of baked goods. That got the twins to leave their tree house and join us at least.

"Maybe we can have a campfire this weekend," Zach said.

"That sounds fun," Lila replied. I said nothing. She nudged my knee with her leg.

"Yeah," Zach said, barreling into my silence, "you should have seen us last time, making s'mores with these giant marshmallows. What a mess, right, Amai?" He leaned forward, trying to catch my eye, but I kept busy peeling the wrapper off a cupcake.

Zach was being so . . . normal. How could he act like the kiss hadn't happened? Did it mean that little to him? The burning embers of hate I'd felt over the last two years burst into red-hot flames.

But soon enough he'd see that every action had consequences.

15

By the next morning, Lila had shaken off her initial shock over Zach's looks and was fully back on task. As we got dressed, she started our revenge game.

"Slash his designer clothes," Lila said as she stepped into a pair of cute cutoffs and tugged them over her pink bikini.

"Run over his sunglasses," I said, pulling on a dress over my blue two-piece and then plopping on a wide-brimmed hat.

"Put glue in his hair product!"

I frowned. That seemed too mean. But I didn't say that out loud. After all, I was the one who wanted him to suffer.

We headed down to eat breakfast on the porch, but Ethan and Mason dragged Lila away halfway through her cereal. I cleaned up and then went to find them, surprised to see Lila up in the tree house. Neither Zach nor I had been invited up there.

Although to be fair, we never let the twins in our fort.

Zach appeared by my side so stealthily that I startled. Our eyes caught, and I quickly looked away.

Zach cleared his throat. "Hey, Amai?" he said, his voice cracking.

I was afraid of what he might say, so I pretended I didn't hear him and instead strode over to the bottom of the platform and called up to the boys, "Hey, you two, give Lila a break. She's on vacation, not babysitting duty."

"Mai said DOODY!" Mason yelled, laughing.

Oh please. That got Ethan going, and soon the boys were singing a song about poop. Lila poked her head out a window and flashed me a grin. "Nice going, Mai!"

I shrugged. "Come on down. We're leaving for the beach in a bit."

We took both cars, my family and Lila in Holly's Accord and the Koyamas in the Pilot.

Once we'd set up our towels on the sand, Lila and I stripped down to our suits and headed for the water. The ocean lapped at our toes.

"It's so warm!" she said.

"Right? Like bathwater!" The Pacific Ocean was chilly, especially where we lived in Northern California. The only time we ever went to the beach was to collect rocks and shells, and we usually wore regular clothes.

We waded farther out until the water was at our waists, the sun beating down on us. I straightened the brim of my hat.

"So will the Hot Pinx audition for the talent show this year?" I asked.

"Hmmm. I hope so. We need to practice a few more covers. The two you heard and maybe another."

"Nice."

Lila ducked into the water to her shoulders. I glanced behind us to where Zach was building a sandcastle with the boys. Lila straightened and followed my gaze.

"We should hang out with Zach," she said. "You know, so he won't be suspicious."

"Yeah. Good idea."

We spent the next hour helping the boys and Zach build the sandcastle, but it quickly turned into a mud splash fight. It felt good to laugh with Lila. I noticed that Zach was quieter than usual, but I was relieved about that. The less talking he did, the better.

After a picnic lunch and a long hike at Bluff Point, we finally wore out the twins. And ourselves. When we got home, while the parents started preparing dinner, I let Lila use the shower first and crashed in my room, accidentally falling asleep.

Their laughter woke me. I didn't know how long I'd been out, but when I got up and peeked out the window, the late-afternoon sun was so bright it made me squint. I blocked the intense light with my hand. Zach and Lila sat on the hammocks talking. I couldn't see their faces from here, but I could tell they were having a good time. Excellent! Lila needed to bond with Zach. And they were overlooking the pond—a perfect opening for her to ask him to take her out in the canoe.

I took my time showering, and after I got dressed, I made my way outside. And now the plan that we'd so carefully crafted was coming together. I swallowed my nerves about spending time with Zach. It was finally happening. I was going to show Zach what it felt like when a friend stabbed you in the back. Maybe then I could finally let him go. I *needed* to let him go. I straightened my shoulders and joined them at the hammocks. Lila smiled and patted the space next to her.

As I sat down, my phone slipped out of my pocket and fell at Zach's feet. He stooped to pick it up before I could. I held out my hand, impatient for him to return it, but he took his time, turning the phone over to look at the case. His eyebrows furrowed.

"Who's this?" he asked, lifting my phone to flash the photo card stashed in the case.

"Jungkook," I said, shaking my hand to get him to give me my phone.

"Oh, yeah," he said, sounding relieved for some reason. "I didn't recognize him at first."

Lila whipped out her phone to show Zach her case with the photo of her bias. "Here's Jimin!"

Zach finally handed me my phone and said, "So, you're still into BTS."

"Um, Zachary," I said, using my best teacher voice, "one never stops loving BTS. It's not a phase to outgrow."

He laughed. "Got it."

"You didn't tell me Zach was into music," Lila said.

"And you didn't tell me Lila has a band," Zach said.

I shrugged, not sure where to go with this. At least they were bonding.

"I showed Lila our fort," Zach added.

I whipped my head so fast to look at him that my hair swished in Lila's face, and I snapped, "*I* was going to take her to our fort!"

Zach raised his hands. "Sorry."

Sorry? That wasn't nearly good enough. This was proof that Zach didn't care about me or my feelings. Lila was *my* best friend. Zach had no right to take her to the fort. I'd been looking forward to showing her around my space.

Zach's eyes flitted to my hands, curled into fists, and he raised his eyebrows in surprise. Just as I was about to blast him for his lack of respect, Lila nudged my knee with hers to remind me to settle down.

I forced a smile while gritting my teeth. Zach's eyebrows stayed raised for a few more seconds until Lila broke the growing silence.

"Mai, you promised you'd show me all the cool birds we don't have in California."

I scanned the trees, relieved to be able to point out a cardinal.

Lila gasped. "I love it! He's so red!"

And though I avoided glancing Zach's way, I heard the hammock creak as he expelled a breath and lay back—in relief, maybe? If he thought he had a reprieve from my anger, he had another thing coming.

I continued identifying birds to Lila while Zach napped in the hammock next to us. But maybe he'd been faking because when Mom called us to dinner, Zach popped right up and dashed to the house.

Lila and I followed. As we entered the backyard, she leaned close to me and whispered, "We are a go! Zach is taking me out in the canoe in the morning."

We hooked pinkies, and I smiled. I was lucky to have Lila as my best friend.

The next morning, I woke up with anticipation fluttering in my stomach. Today was the big day. Revenge Day. Lila and I kept bursting out in giggles as we got dressed. Then, before breakfast, we pumped ourselves up by dancing to BTS. Lila wasn't into choreography like I was, but she had great rhythm (of course) and danced along with me.

Zach joined us on the porch, wearing cargo shorts and a gray T-shirt and looking more like the Zach I used to know. It would be just the three of us this morning. Wes, Mom, and Holly had already taken the boys to the aquarium, and Dad was working.

After we ate, I helped Zach carry the canoe to the water and held it steady as Lila got in, taking my seat. Her grin was catching, and I smiled, too. No doubt Zach thought she was excited to go out on the pond. Maybe she was a little, but I knew the true joy came from putting my plan into action.

Zach climbed into the back of the canoe and glanced at me. "I'll take you out after," he said.

I shook my head. "It's okay. This is a special treat for Lila. We can go another time." I didn't want Zach to rush back for me. I wanted to have plenty of time to find his phone and upload the pics to his account. Besides, I never wanted to canoe with him again.

"Have fun," I said.

"We will!" Zach grinned.

I grinned back at him, and he widened his eyes in surprise, looking pleased. There wasn't one part of me that felt bad for my deception. He deserved to get a big taste of his own sour medicine.

I waited until they were out in the middle of the pond before I forced myself to walk casually back to the house.

But once I was out of sight, all bets were off. My heart hammered, matching the rhythm of my feet pounding up the stairs, and my clenched fists were moist with sweat. When I got to Zach's room, I grabbed the door frame to take a steadying breath. I'd waited a very long time for this moment. I wanted to savor the sweet taste of my victory.

The twins' side of the room truly looked like a tornado had hit it. Clothes were scattered everywhere, along with plastic dinosaurs and LEGO bricks of every size and color.

I turned my attention to Zach's side. He'd been a messy kid, too, but was neater these days. His bed was made, and his nightstand was stacked with travel books.

I pulled out my phone and tapped on the folder of embarrassing photos of Zach I'd been collecting, then scanned his nightstand. His phone wasn't there. But I was good at finding things. Years of birdwatching had sharpened my skills. Yet after a quick circuit, I didn't see it. A trickle of dread threaded through me.

I hurried downstairs and looked around the kitchen, the living room, and then the porch. No! Where was it? I squinted at the pond. Lila and Zach were all the way on the far side. I had to find it before they ran out of things to talk about and turned back for home.

I forced myself to relax. Then I checked the couch cushions, the floor, and the bathrooms. No phone.

I ran back to Zach's room and dialed his number. I wondered if he still used the Super Mario Bros. ringtone. Probably not. Spinning around his room, I listened for a ringing phone. Just as I was about to hang up and try again downstairs, Zach picked up.

He.

Picked.

Up!

"Amai? Is everything okay?"

No, everything was not okay! I could totally imagine Lila's face as she realized Zach had his phone on him. Our plan had failed. *I* had failed.

"Oops," I said, thinking quickly. "I hit the wrong number. And why do you have your phone anyway?"

Zach laughed. "I forgot! Don't tell Dad I took it with me."

He forgot? "Um . . . okay, I won't," I said, and hung up before he noticed how weird I was being.

In my room, I paced with the AC on full blast and tried to keep myself from bawling. I wanted to lie down on the floor and flail like a toddler. The perfect plan blown to bits. It wasn't fair!

Through the window, I saw Zach and Lila over by the birch trees. He and Lila were peering down over the side of the canoe. Maybe they saw a turtle. I sighed, feeling like nothing mattered anymore. I used the time I had left to calm down. But by the time they returned to shore, I was still filled with heavy disappointment.

At dinner, it became clear that my opportunity to get Zach's phone and embarrass him in front of his friends was lost. He and Wes were heading to Fairfield that evening and would return with Celeste and Noah in the morning. When I'd invited them, I'd been sure that Lila and I would have completed our mission successfully by then, which would mean Celeste and Noah—along with the rest of Zach's thousands of Instagram followers—would have already seen his embarrassing photos, and I'd get to watch their reactions and gloat. But there was no chance of that now. And even though, originally, I thought it would be great for Lila to meet Celeste, now I was just annoyed to lose precious time with Lila.

As we got ready for bed, she tried to cheer me up. "Oh, Mai. I know you're bummed, but it isn't the end of the world."

"But it is!"

"We might get another chance to upload the photos when he comes back with his friends."

"Nope. He hardly ever lets his phone out of his sight," I said. "It's over."

"You have the rest of the summer."

I shrugged.

"Come on, Mai." Lila sat on my bed where I was curled up on my side. "It's going to be okay."

I sighed. Early in seventh grade, Lila had lost first chair for the cello in orchestra. She had been really upset, but after maybe an hour of wallowing, she'd rebounded with determination and optimism. I didn't know how she did that, how she could let go of her disappointment so easily. I was the opposite. I shoved my feelings way down deep.

Besides, Lila won back first chair a couple of weeks later. It seemed like everyone got what they wanted but me.

Lila and I only had one more full day together before she flew home without me. I wanted to go with her. When I was with Lila, everything was good.

"Forget about Zach," I said. "Let's just have fun tomorrow."

Making some happy memories with Lila was all I had left. And I'd hold on to them to get me through the next three weeks until we could be together again.

16

Lila and I spent the next morning in the hammocks, talking about her band and Alex, and listening to new music. We were interrupted by a familiar text tone. I checked my phone and smiled.

Celeste
We are in the car and on our way!

Mai
Great! See you soon!

Noah
Zach and I challenge you three to a cornhole tournament.
Winners get to choose the pizza topping.

Zach
Good. I want sausage and pepperoni.

Celeste

Gross! Veggie pizza bc we are going to win!

"What's up?" Lila asked.

"Celeste and the guys are on their way."

"Oh."

I glanced up at Lila. "You'll like Celeste. I promise."

Lila smiled. "I'm sure I will."

Lila probably felt a little like I did—possessive of our time together. But it wasn't like I could disinvite Celeste and Noah.

Just then, an unfamiliar car pulled into the driveway. It was Margie from the nature center!

"Hi, Mai!" she greeted me. "Is now a good time to look at the property?"

"Sure," I said. "Holly's out, but I can show you around."

I introduced her to Lila, then led them both along the trail to the clearing and showed them where I'd found the owl pellets. I'd been checking regularly but hadn't found any more.

After she examined the area thoroughly, she asked to see inside the garage. Lila and I waited in the driveway. When Margie finally came out to join us, she was smiling.

"Well, Mai, I'm impressed with your birding skills," she said as we walked to her car. "I do believe you may have or at least had a barn owl roosting in the garage. I saw some down feathers and found an old pellet. I hope you don't mind if I take it with me."

"That's fine." I said. On the outside, I played it cool, but inside, I was bursting with excitement. We might have a barn owl!

Margie opened the door to her truck. "Do me a favor, Mai, and if you happen to spot the barn owl, let me know?" She handed me her card. "You can go to our website for tips on how and when to look for owls."

"I will!" I clutched her card to my chest, hoping I'd see it more than anything.

We waved goodbye to Margie, but before we had a chance to head back in the house, another car pulled up. Zach, Noah, and Celeste piled out of the Pilot. Celeste headed straight for us while Zach and Noah ambled, taking their time. Now I'd have to share my time with Lila.

"Hi!" Celeste nearly stuck her face in Lila's. "I'm so happy to meet Mai's BFF!"

Lila smiled and greeted her. Zach joined us and introduced Noah.

"Who's ready to lose to the cornhole champs?" Noah joked.

"You wish," Celeste said. "It's girls versus boys. Prepare to be destroyed . . . again!"

I schooled Lila on how to play cornhole while the others got the boards set up. We girls alternated in for three games, and we beat the guys every time. Celeste and I taught Lila our victory dance. Fortunately the guys were actually good sports.

Dad and Wes picked up Nana's tomato pies for dinner: two with our choice of veggie toppings and a sausage pizza for the guys because Celeste was a gracious winner. Mason and Ethan begged to join us because they wanted to be with Lila. They wanted to sit with her at every meal. Fortunately, after Lila promised to sit with them at breakfast the next morning, they relented. The five of us set up chairs by the pond to share the three pizzas.

As we were about to sit down, Zach noticed Lila's drumsticks as she removed them from her back pocket. She hadn't taken them in the canoe, fearful they'd fall into the water.

"I wanted to take drum lessons in Tokyo," Zach said. "Actually it was for the Japanese taiko drum, but Mom wouldn't let me because she was afraid the twins would also want to learn and then she'd be listening to drumming forever."

We laughed.

Lila twirled her drumsticks and handed them to Zach, and they took seats next to each other. My stomach rolled at the sight of Lila's precious drumsticks in Zach's hands.

I took a bite of my pizza, chewing silently, listening to Zach and Lila jabber away. Relief filled me when Zach handed back Lila's drumsticks.

"What's your band like?" Zach asked, his slice of pizza still on his plate in his lap. Usually he would have been on his second slice by now.

"The Hot Pinx? We're coming along."

"That is a kick-butt name!" Zach shouted. "What kind of music?"

I turned to Celeste, talking loud enough to try to drown out Zach and Lila's conversation, which turned to some of the bands Zach loved from Japan. "Do you like music?"

Celeste nibbled on a pizza crust. "Yeah, but not obsessively like Zach."

"Hey!" Zach chimed in. "I'm not obsessed!"

"Yeah," Noah said, laughing. "You are!"

"Amai! Tell these people I've got other interests, too!"

Everyone turned to me, smiling.

Zach gently shoved Noah. "At least Amai's always got my back."

My smile dissolved. Without answering, I leaned back in my chair, scanning the pond for wildlife. When it became apparent I wasn't going to respond, Zach and Lila continued their music conversation, hardly missing a beat. Lila even showed Zach (and, okay, everyone else) the videos of her band. Zach watched a second and then a third time, all the while raving. I mean, yeah, I totally agreed with him, but give it a rest already!

After watching the video the first time, Celeste returned to her seat next to me. "Wow, Lila is super talented."

"Right? She plays the cello for our school orchestra and drums in the band. She can play any instrument after only a few practice sessions."

"You must hate her just a little."

"What? No!"

Celeste widened her eyes. "I was joking. Sorry. Noah teases me that I'm not as funny as I think I am."

I'd probably reacted too strongly because I was getting more and more annoyed by the way Lila and Zach continued to connect over music. Didn't Lila believe me when I said I was done trying to get Zach back, at least while she was here? I wanted to spend time with *her*.

Just then, she waved to me. "Mai! You have to listen to these bands Zach got into while he was living in Japan. The band names are totally fab: Dustcell, Radwimps, Band-Maid, and this all-girl rock band, Scandal!"

I couldn't stand watching my former BFF and my current BFF hit it off anymore. I mean, Lila had waited till now to share any of the Hot Pinx music with me but showed virtual strangers her videos immediately? What was up with that?

"I'm going to head into the house," I said to no one in particular, but Celeste leapt up next to me.

"I'll go with you," she said. "I mean, I like music as much as the next person, but those two, and even Noah, are mad into it."

"Do you feel like baking cookies?" I asked as she followed me toward the house. It was a cool day for once, and I wouldn't melt if I turned on the oven.

"I love baking!" Celeste said. "We can surprise the others."

The minute we started to measure and mix, Ethan and Mason came charging into the kitchen. Fortunately it was the one place the boys settled down. They loved to "help," and Holly had made it very clear they were not allowed to goof off around any of the appliances.

Celeste and I let Ethan and Mason scoop the chocolate chip cookie dough onto the baking sheets. Then we played a quick game of Uno with the boys while the cookies were in the oven. When they were ready, we piled some on a plate for the twins to take to their tree house. I left a second plate on the counter for the parents, and Celeste and I carried the last plate outside, where we found Noah and Zach playing cornhole again. I grabbed two cookies and made a beeline for Lila, who was curled up on the hammock.

"Your favorite," I said, holding one out to her.

She took it and flashed me a smile that I knew wasn't real. Did Zach say something to upset her? Anger simmered. Forget sneaking humiliation, I'd outright yell at him if he hurt Lila!

"What's wrong?" I asked.

"You disappeared. You could have invited me to bake cookies, too," she said, her voice wavering.

Oh. *I* hurt her. Something I'd never done to my best friend before.

"I'm sorry," I said. "I thought you were having fun with Zach. You know, talking about music and stuff."

I tried to keep my voice light, but Lila knew me too well. She peered at me. "You're upset!"

"No, I'm not." I took a giant bite of cookie and chewed vigorously.

"I didn't mean to get so wrapped up in the conversation," Lila said. "But it was really cool learning about Japanese rock bands."

I continued nibbling at my cookie.

"I would never betray your friendship, Mai. You hate Zach, so I do, too."

"Do you?"

"Okay, well, maybe *hate* is a strong word. I don't like that he treated you badly. But that was two years ago."

I narrowed my eyes at her. "What are you saying?"

Lila raised her hands, holding up her untouched cookie. "It's nothing."

"Look," I tried again. "I should have invited you inside with us." Lila didn't like baking, but now didn't seem like a good time to remind her of that.

She shrugged.

"Are you upset about something else?"

"I didn't like seeing you go off with Celeste. It made me feel like you'd rather spend time with her. Like maybe you're ready for me to go home and leave you to your summer friends."

"Oh, Lila." I gripped her hand. "I'm sorry!" I totally understood her jealousy. I kind of felt the same about her spending all her time with Iris and the others.

Lila snapped her cookie in half, and crumbs fell to the grass below. Her expression was so sad that it broke my heart. I'd never put that look on her face before. Ever. And I never wanted to do that again.

"Lila." I leaned my head on her shoulder. "I'm really sorry I hurt your feelings. I promise, you have nothing to worry about with Celeste. She's not really my friend, at least, not like you are. Remember our plan? I was using her to get dirt on Zach. That's all! And I admit I was jealous of how you and Zach were getting along. So I took off with Celeste."

Lila sighed. "Okay. I mean, I get it. We both had parts to play. You had to fake a friendship with Celeste, and I had to pretend to like Zach. But that's all over with, right?"

"Right! You and me, we're the real deal. BFFs. We have history!"

"Remember the time we were drinking boba tea and you were

swooning over that pic of Jungkook and I made that face?" Lila started giggling. She sucked in her cheeks and made fish lips while crossing her eyes.

"I burst out laughing and spit out my tea." I giggled along with her.

"And the tapioca ball flew out of your mouth and hit me on the forehead and—" Lila gasped as she laughed.

Suddenly everything seemed hysterical. "And it bounced off your forehead and almost back into my mouth." My stomach hurt from laughing.

"I wish I could stay longer," Lila said once we'd caught our breath.

"I wish you could, too, but then you'd miss Alex." I nudged her with my shoulder.

"Then I wish you could come back home."

"Me too." I felt a little better. "Three more weeks, Lila. We can do this. I'll be home soon enough."

We turned to each other, and she held out her pinkie. "Stay gold."

I hooked mine with hers. "Stay gold."

I noticed a flutter of movement, and I swung around to see Zach walking up to us.

"Hey, my dad's getting ready to take Noah and Celeste home."

Zach tried to catch my eye, but my glance skittered away to the driveway, where his friends were loading their bags into the Pilot.

He sighed loudly. "Anyway, I guess I'll go with them. Give you two time to hang out together. Dad has a meeting tomorrow, so we won't be back until after it's over. It was nice meeting you, Lila."

Zach's eyes rested on me, a question in his eyes as Lila said good-bye. I glanced down at my feet. A long few seconds later, he headed to the car.

Zach wanted to talk to me about something but knew I wouldn't with Lila here. She was my buffer. And now that she was leaving, I'd have to figure out how to avoid any conversation with him for the next three weeks. I may not have been able to get revenge on him—though I'd still try if the opportunity showed up—but that didn't mean I could forgive and forget. Zach had spent most of lunch monopolizing Lila. And that comment about my having his back stirred up all the ugly memories. Why should I have his back when he so obviously didn't have mine? One thing was for sure, I was done pretending to be friends with him.

17

Lila and I stopped at the car where Zach, Noah, and Celeste were waiting for Wes to come out.

"Thanks for coming," I said to Noah and Celeste.

"It was fun!" Noah said.

Celeste had ducked her head into the back of the Pilot to dig around in her bag. She might not have heard me, but before I could give her a hug and say a proper goodbye, Lila grabbed my arm and tugged me toward the house. We passed Wes as he headed to the car.

I was so glad to have Lila to myself again for the evening. Mom said we could eat dinner in the backyard while everyone else ate on the porch. One thing about Mom and Holly's friendship was that it meant she totally understood that I wanted to spend time alone with my BFF.

While Lila went up to our room to snag a hoodie, I headed to the kitchen for some drinks. I grabbed a pitcher of lemonade and was just about to pour when I noticed Noah had left his hat. Snagging it, I ran out to the driveway. Dad and Wes were talking at the car, but I didn't see anyone else. If Zach had taken everyone to the fort, I was going to be super annoyed. I stalked over to the path but stopped short when I heard voices, triggering the memory of another conversation I wasn't meant to hear. Curiosity won over self-preservation, and I leaned in to listen.

"Mai's a liar and a fake!"

Celeste's voice was full of anger. It sounded like she was crying.

"CeCe, I'm sure you're wrong," Zach said.

"I know what I heard!" Celeste said. "Mai told Lila she was using me! And you should watch out because they're using you, too!"

I blinked in shock. Celeste had overheard my conversation with Lila on the hammock.

Zach's voice was calm and soothing. "Mai isn't like that. She's like the nicest person I know."

"You're biased," Celeste said, sniffling. "Plus, maybe she's changed. It's been like two years since you last saw her."

"Maybe," Zach admitted. "But I think I know Mai. She wouldn't do something like that. Just talk to her. Give her a chance to explain."

Oh, *now* Zach defends me?

"It doesn't matter," Celeste said. "It's not like we were really friends; that much is clear. I'll never see her again anyway."

I backed away and ran, shoving Noah's hat at Wes on my way to the house. My chest ached knowing that I'd hurt Celeste's feelings. I would never have said any of that if I thought she would hear me. It wasn't like I truly meant it—I had only been trying to soothe Lila.

Forget everything you just heard, I told myself as I walked back to the house. I was used to this, trying to bury the feelings I didn't know how to handle. But I couldn't get Celeste's hurt voice out of my head. Her words replayed over and over in a loop. I knew I should run out to the driveway before she left so I could apologize. If only she hadn't overheard me! Saying what you thought people wanted to hear never ended well. I knew that better than anyone.

Lost in thought, I barely noticed Lila coming back downstairs. She smiled at me. "Dinner with my best friend," she said, her voice light and full of joy.

Right. My priority was Lila. She'd be leaving too soon. I hooked my arm in hers and led her to the backyard, where Mom had a table set with our dinner. I glanced at the driveway. The Pilot was gone.

After dinner and dessert, Lila and I borrowed Mom's laptop and watched our favorite episodes of *Run BTS!* The time flew. Mom reminded us that we had an early morning, so we headed up to my room.

I was quiet as we got ready for bed. My thoughts kept wandering to Celeste as we climbed under the covers, but I pushed the guilt away and snapped off the light.

"Mai? Everything okay?" Lila asked softly.

I rubbed my eyes. "Sorry. Yes, everything is okay. Well, as okay as it can be." I was going to miss her. "I wish I could go home with you."

"I wish you could, too." Lila rustled around in bed and sat up. "Hey, Mai?"

"Hmm?"

"I think you should be honest with Zach."

I sat up slowly, careful not to hit my head. "What do you mean?"

Lila finger-combed her hair, a nervous habit. "Just that maybe you should talk to him about what you heard him say two years ago."

I thought about Celeste overhearing me. Even if she'd confronted me like Zach had suggested, I wasn't sure what I could have said to make her feel better. I mean, I could have apologized for sure, but thinking back to what Zach had done, an apology right after wouldn't have changed how betrayed I'd felt. No, an apology alone wasn't enough. I wanted to know why he'd been so mean and uncaring. I thought about how upset Celeste was and how new our friendship was. What I'd done was unforgivable. That thought sat like a stone in my stomach.

"It's too late."

"I don't know," Lila said. "I mean, you two were close once. Don't you miss that?"

"Are you trying to get rid of me?" I asked, trying to make a joke.

"Of course not!" Lila sighed. "I know you're not thrilled that Zach and I hung out, but, Mai, the way he talks about you! I can't believe that he doesn't care about you. Maybe he made a mistake back then."

"He doesn't care about me!" I snapped.

Lila got quiet. She lay back down, tugging the covers up to her chin. Great. Not only did I hurt Celeste's feelings but now I'd hurt Lila's. Again. What was wrong with me? I was better than this. I knew what a best friend was, even if Zach didn't. It meant being loyal for sure but also kind. And I also knew that meant I couldn't keep secrets from Lila.

"He kissed me," I said quietly.

"What?" Lila screeched, and then sat up so quickly she hit her head. "Ow! When? When did he kiss you?"

"The afternoon you arrived. Before Mom and I picked you up."

"Holy drumsticks, Mai! Why did you wait till now to tell me?"

"I don't know."

"Tell me everything!"

She sounded so happy, so excited. But this wasn't something to be celebrated. It wasn't like her kiss with Alex. It was . . . it was a mistake.

"Mai?"

"There's nothing to tell." There was nothing between me and Zach. "Don't sound so happy, Lila. You know better."

Even in the dim light, I could see a flash of hurt flare on her face. Again. I counted out the seconds of silence.

"Okay," Lila said. "Did he like force it on you? Because if he did, that's all kinds of wrong."

I shook my head. As much as I'd like for Zach to be the villain in this story, I couldn't lie. "No. I mean, it was kind of mutual."

"Kind of?" Her voice held a drop of hope. And when I didn't answer, she went on. "Mai, clearly there's something between you two. This confirms what I was saying earlier. You should talk to him about what happened two years ago. It might all be a big misunderstanding."

"How can Zach not defending me to two racists be a misunderstanding?"

"I don't know. Mai, we all make mistakes."

My thoughts flickered once again to Celeste.

"Your first kiss with Zach, Mai. That has to mean something."

I had nothing to say to that, especially since technically it wasn't our first kiss. I didn't want to think about what this one meant. Didn't want it to mean anything at all.

After another drawn-out silence, Lila said quietly, "I don't think you really hate him like you say you do."

"But I do, Lila. I really, really do!" I threw myself back down on my bed and turned toward the wall. "Let's just go to sleep."

Lila lay down and pulled the covers over her. And in moments, I heard her slow, even breaths. She'd always been able to fall asleep quickly.

I, on the other hand, lay awake for a long time, replaying an old memory I'd rather have forgotten.

Sweet

SIX SUMMERS AGO

Zach held the hammock steady, but my short seven-year-old legs didn't quite reach as I tried and failed to climb in. I thought that maybe he'd laugh and tease me like I often teased him. Instead, Zach trekked off to the other side of the apple orchard.

He came back dragging the stepladder Wes used to trim the branches of the trees.

"Be careful, Amai," he said, holding the hammock again.

I stepped onto the ladder and rolled into the hammock, ungracefully, my legs flying straight up as I gripped the edges so I didn't tumble off the other side.

"You did it!" Zach cheered. He moved the stepladder and easily flipped onto the hammock next to me.

I hung on as it swayed. Once I felt like I wouldn't fall off, I relaxed, looking up at the leafy branches and the blue sky. I'd been wanting to sit in Mom's hammock all summer and finally, on the last day, here I was.

"Thanks, Zach," I said, smiling at him.

Zach's face was right next to mine as he turned to me. "I'm going to miss you."

"Me too. But I'll be back next summer."

"I'm glad." Zach's eyes lit up with his smile.

I was happy we felt the same about spending time together. My joy bubbled over, making my heart full of gladness. I leaned over and kissed him on the lips.

"Ahhhh!" Zach jerked away in surprise, making the hammock swing wildly.

I tumbled out of the hammock onto the soft lawn below me.

Zach peered over the hammock, reaching out a hand to me. "Amai! Are you okay?"

I laughed as I let him pull me back up. We settled in, shoulder to shoulder, as we relaxed in the gently swaying hammock. I sighed happily, thinking, *Friends forever.*

18

"Mai must be really upset about Lila leaving," Mom told Holly. "She hasn't said a word since we got back from the airport, and she's been holed up in her room all day."

I really did need to let the parents know their voices carried from the back porch. I closed my window. It wasn't hot enough to turn on the AC, so I flipped the switch for my ceiling fan and lay back down, letting the air waft over me.

Zach and Wes had returned a couple of hours ago. Not that I cared. What I did care about was that Lila was gone and I was stuck here, alone. I cared that things had felt a little off between us ever since we'd gone to sleep the night before. I hadn't wanted to argue with Lila about the kiss and about Zach.

But not arguing was almost the same as not talking. Lila had hardly spoken to me this morning. I mean, we'd had to get up super early to go to the airport and were both sleepy. Still, when we parted at the gate, we hadn't hooked pinkies and instead just gave each other an awkward hug.

I checked my phone again—it would be another hour until her plane landed in San Francisco, and then another hour after that till she was home in Sunnyvale.

"Mai? Come on down for dinner," Dad called.

I contemplated saying I was too tired or not hungry, but that would probably cause more grief than just sucking it up and being in Zach's presence. I'd done it up till now; I could suffer for a few more weeks.

When I got to the porch, Ethan and Mason ran over to me, tugging me toward the dinner table. Now that Lila was gone, they were back to fighting over who got to sit with me.

"You two are fickle," I said, pushing a chair between them.

"I'm a pickle!" Mason shouted with glee.

"No, I said *fickle*."

"That means you aren't loyal," Zach explained.

I shot Zach a glare. "Yeah. Exactly."

His eyebrows shot up.

"We're sorry," Mason said, hugging my arm. "We love you, Mai-nesan! Daisukidesu."

I dragged my eyes away from Zach's and patted Mason's head. "I know. It's okay. I forgive you."

"Me too?" Ethan asked.

I draped an arm around each twin. "Yes. I forgive you both." But not Zach. Never Zach. What he had done was unforgivable.

When we were finally finished with dinner, I was glad it was Zach's turn to clean up. While he did the dishes, I sat at the table and joined in the conversation just long enough to make everyone think all was well. Then I went straight to my room. Sitting in front of my closed door was a small bag. My gift from Zach. Like that would change anything. I snatched it and tossed it onto Lila's bed, now stripped of sheets. My heart ached. I was homesick.

My eyes filled with tears, and I swiped them away with the back of my hand. Then I sat on my bed and pulled out my phone. Still no messages from Lila.

Mai

Hey, did you get home safe & sound? IMY

I stared at my screen. Nothing. No read receipt or telltale dots. Maybe she wasn't home yet. I counted back the three-hour time difference. Maybe she was having a late lunch with her parents, or unpacking, or having band practice, or seeing Alex. I'd check later.

But later came and still nothing from Lila. I tried again.

No answer.

I pretty much stared at my phone for the next hour, hoping Lila would reach out, but she didn't. Was she mad at me? In the two years that she and I have been best friends, we had never had a fight. I wasn't even sure we were fighting now, but we'd left things sort of weird. It made my skin feel all itchy and tight.

I heard Holly put the twins to bed. Now the parents would sit on the porch and play cards. Dad would stay up late, working. I just wanted this summer to be over.

Peering out the window, I saw that it was starting to get dark. I'd read that this was a great time to spot owls—when it was still light enough for me to see as they got more active, preparing to hunt for the night.

"Take Zach with you," Mom said when I told the parents where I was going.

I rolled my eyes. "I'm going to be right by the garage. I'll be perfectly safe and won't stay out too long."

I could tell Mom wanted to insist, but she nodded. It was so annoying that everyone thought Zach and I had to be joined at the hip. I didn't need to do everything with him. I didn't want to do anything with him.

I slipped away from the porch, leaving the parents to their card game. Walking through the backyard and out the gate, I followed the driveway to the garage. The light was on in our fort. As I stealthily snuck past, I could hear Zach's music playing. I knew he wasn't dancing. In all the years I'd known him, he'd never liked it. But he'd always kept me company as I learned choreography. When I put on a show, Zach cheered and applauded.

I checked my phone one more time. Still nothing from Lila. She was definitely home by now. Was she ignoring me? Was she annoyed that I didn't want to follow her advice and give Zach a chance? Maybe she'd decided I was too stubborn to bother with. Ugh! But I couldn't think about that now. I needed to focus if I wanted to spot the barn owl.

I made it to the clearing without seeing an owl or hearing its telltale screech. Sighing quietly, I sat on my stump and slumped.

In the still of the evening, I watched the sky change from orange to lavender to dusky blue. The night burst into a symphony as crickets and cicadas sang soprano, punctuated from time to time with the low bass of a bullfrog. Even listening to nature's music made me miss Lila.

And that made me think of Zach, as much as I didn't want to. After a couple of weeks of getting along with Zach and feeling like things might be back to normal, the distance between us now felt like a canyon. One I'd never be able to cross again.

I kicked my heels against my stump and glared at Zach's empty one. Memories started to play out in front of me like a movie montage. Zach and I had spent many hours over many summers sitting in this clearing. It was where he told me he didn't want to join the baseball team in sixth grade. Where I'd told him I stanned BTS and he hadn't made fun of me. I saw my first downy woodpecker while sitting here with him, three years ago. And I'd danced to many a song with Zach as my audience of one.

In the safety of the dark, in what used to be my favorite place in the world, I risked opening my heart just the slightest sliver and allowed myself to remember how strange it felt not getting on a flight last July. Good thing I'd had Lila by then. But something had been missing. That first week of July, a big box had arrived in the mail. It was addressed to Mom, but I'd recognized the handwriting and saw the return address label, from Holly. Even though I had been so angry at Zach for the last year, now that we were apart for the first summer ever, I kind of sort of missed him.

That evening, as a family, we opened that box. Mom pulled out a note addressed from Holly and read it with a smile on her face. They emailed and video chatted regularly, but a real letter was nice. Holly wanted to do our traditional gift exchange even though we couldn't be together. Mom passed out the gifts to me and Dad. Japanese snacks and an adorable realistic plush rabbit for me. After we were done, I stuck my head in the box, searching for the apology note from Zach that Mom must have missed. But there was nothing else in there.

"Mai," Mom had said. "Don't be so sad. I know it's not the same as being together, but this is the next best thing."

As usual, Mom couldn't cope with me being upset. It wasn't the next best thing. But Mom might be onto something. Bad feelings were a waste of time, and so was a friendship with Zach. I had missed him, but not anymore. He had been my very best friend for my whole life. Until he wasn't. And the longer we went without talking, the truer that became.

I blinked myself back to the present. I couldn't stand the thought of losing Lila the same way. I didn't know if we were okay. I was scared that a summer apart would change us, would change our friendship the way it had changed mine and Zach's. If he and I had had our summer together, would it have been easier to talk to him about what I'd heard? I'd never know. What I did know was I couldn't lose another best friend.

Slowly the tears came. The weight of my sadness and loneliness pressed down on me, making it hard to breathe. I hated feeling this kind of pain, the kind that twisted and squeezed in my chest. When you got a cut, you might bleed, but the pain faded quickly. You stuck a Band-Aid on, and it healed. This kind of pain never healed. It ached and throbbed. And no matter how hard I tried to bury it, it flared up at unexpected times.

And it hurt.

I muffled my sobs with my hands and willed myself to stop.

When I finally lifted my head, night had fallen. The stars blazed in the sky, reminding me of the fireworks I had seen with Lila, and fresh tears pooled in my eyes.

Finally I scrubbed at my face, forcing myself to calm down. I used the hem of my shirt to wipe my eyes and nose, then stood and took a deep steadying breath. I needed to make it back to my room without anyone seeing me, especially my parents. They couldn't handle sadness any better than I could.

I'd take a long shower and go to sleep. And I wouldn't look at my phone for text messages from Lila. My heart couldn't take any more rejection.

If only I could wave a magic wand and make everything better. Zach would have never betrayed me. Lila wouldn't be upset with me. This would be the best summer of my life, but I'd still be looking forward to my life back home.

I stared at my feet. Maybe all wasn't lost. Lila seemed to think somehow things *could* get better if I let them. I wanted to believe her. I just needed a sign, one that would give me hope.

I glanced back up at the stars one more time and froze.

Something white flew right over my head, so close I could almost reach up and touch it. It didn't make any noise as it swooped past me, its wings spread in silent flight.

It was the barn owl.

It was hope.

19

Noah

Yo, I know Z's not coming back this weekend, but we on for weekend after?

Zach

If you all are still up for Mai's b-day party, yes!

Noah

You know it! My mom has to be in RI so she'll drop us off.

Zach

Noah

CeCe? You coming, right?

Celeste

No.

Noah

Aw come on C. It will be fun.

Celeste

I told you I'm done with Mai.
She's a fake!
She prob was laughing at me all along.
Poor CeCe has no friends.
I was a big joke.

Zach

C will you just talk to her?
It's got to be a misunderstanding.

Noah

Please C?

Zach

The party will be fun.
I'll make it worth your while.
I have a surprise.

Celeste

Um, guys?

Noah

???

Celeste

This is our other group chat.
The one w Mai on it.

I waited to see if anyone would text anything else, but the chat went silent. No doubt they switched to whatever group chat they had thought they'd been on.

I read the thread twice more. I'd known Celeste thought I was playing her, but to be able to see clearly the anger and hurt in her own words made it harder to ignore. The more I thought about how upset Celeste was, the more sick to my stomach I felt.

I liked Noah and Celeste. And I really had considered Celeste a friend. She was so honest and upbeat. As much as I wanted to pretend that I didn't care, I knew I was lying to myself. I'd blown my friendship with her by saying something mean. And even though I'd only been trying to soothe Lila, that was no excuse.

Then I noticed that Lila had texted me last night after I'd fallen asleep.

Lila
Got home safe!
Mom & Dad kept me busy until now.
Talk tomorrow.

I was filled with relief. Lila wasn't ignoring me. She wasn't avoiding me. I glanced at the time. It was still too early to call her.

I'd asked for a sign last night and seen my first barn owl. It had given me hope, but I was a realist. Things wouldn't magically get fixed. If I wanted this icky feeling of guilt and regret to go away, I had to do the work. I started a new text thread.

I got a read receipt immediately. I waited a few long seconds and then got a response.

Celeste

Sure.

I called her, and she picked up on the first ring.

"I want to apologize," I said. Celeste didn't say anything, but I could hear her breathing. "I know you overheard me talking about you with Lila. Not that it excuses what I said, but I was trying to make Lila feel better. She was a little jealous that you and I had baked together without inviting her along."

Still, Celeste said nothing, so I barreled on. "Again, not that it makes it okay, but I didn't mean it. I do think of you as a friend. I wasn't using you. I mean, I did hope you would share something to help me get revenge on Zach, but I really do like you and want to be friends."

Celeste gasped. "Revenge on Zach? What do you mean?"

Oh shoot! I hadn't meant to let that slip!

"It doesn't matter. Not anymore. The only thing that matters is that I was wrong. I'm really sorry, Celeste."

I strained to hear the sound of her breathing. Had she ended the call?

"CeCe," she said. "My friends call me CeCe."

I let out a big sigh of relief. "Does that mean you forgive me?"

"I'm glad you called and apologized. It's not worth all the negative energy to stay angry. My feelings were definitely hurt, but holding a grudge only makes it worse. Kind of like that saying about adding fuel to the fire."

Celeste reminded me of Lila that way—she was able to let go of bad feelings so easily. How did she do that? Not that I didn't appreciate it.

"Thanks," I said to Celeste. "I hope we can be friends again."

"I totally don't know how friendships work."

"Nobody does. I mean, at least I don't. I'm just making it up as I go, doing the best I can." It was the truth. I wasn't an expert on friendships. Look at me and Zach. "I made a mistake, Celeste. I'm sorry."

"We're good. Thanks for calling. I was spending way too much time making up stories in my head about how you were laughing at me for being friendless."

"I wasn't. I wouldn't. Besides you aren't friendless. You have Noah and Zach and all those guys. And you have me."

"Awesome," Celeste said softly with a smile in her voice. Then she cleared her throat. "So, what's this about revenge?"

"Oh, nothing. It was stupid," I said.

"So you're not mad at Zach?"

Oh, I was definitely mad at Zach, but I didn't want to discuss this with her. We may have patched things up, but she was Zach's friend first.

"Don't break his heart, Mai," Celeste said, sounding serious.

"What are you talking about?"

"How Zach feels. You do know, right?"

"Know what?"

"He looooves you." She laughed.

My heart nearly stopped right then and there. "He does not!"

"Well, he sure acts like it. He talks about you all the time. I knew almost everything about you by the time we met. Right before school ended, Noah teased him so hard about you. He told Zach to just get it off his chest and write you a love letter. I think this summer was his love letter to you."

I sputtered, "Wh-wh-what?"

"He planned all those gifts for you that he bought in Japan. You should have heard him going on and on about which ones he was going to give you in what order. The hours he spent agonizing! It was sweet."

My mind was spinning. I mean, of course Celeste was totally off base. She had to be. Zach didn't care about me at all. He'd just given me those gifts because that's what our families did. They didn't change the fact that he'd betrayed our friendship.

"Anyway, I'm stoked for your birthday party. I can't wait to see what Zach got for you. He won't tell me or Noah anything about it other than we have to be at your party if we want to know."

"Oh, uh, yeah." I didn't even know what I was saying. Time to change the subject. To anything else. "We're good, right?" I asked.

"Yes."

At least I'd fixed that.

"Mai? I have to go! Noah's on his way over, but I'll see you at your party!"

She hung up, and minutes later, I was still sitting there with the phone in my hand, confused by what Celeste had said.

20

After a long while, I stood and stretched, cracking my back. Then I remembered the gift bag on the bed. Celeste said Zach had agonized over the gifts and the order he'd give them to me.

I tore open the bag and dumped it upside down onto the mattress, and out fell a small flat box. It wasn't wrapped like the other gifts from Japan. Inside was a folded piece of paper.

Look under your bed. –Z

I dropped to my knees and peeked. A larger flat package lay hidden halfway toward the wall. I pulled it out, and as I unwrapped it, the paper fell away and my heart leapt with recognition of seven very familiar, very adored faces. It was a framed picture of BTS on the cover of a Japanese magazine—a photo I hadn't seen before.

I snatched up my phone, snapped a pic of it, and sent it to Lila.

Mai
OMG! Look what I got from Zach!

Lila
Holy drumsticks!
That's amazing! I'm jelly!

Mai
Right?
I can't believe Zach went through the trouble of framing it for me!

My phone rang with a FaceTime request from Lila.

"Lila!" My heart swelled, seeing her smiling face.

"Mai!"

We stared at each other for a few beats.

"I miss you," I said, blinking my eyes quickly to keep any tears from falling. "I don't want you to be mad at me."

"Oh, Mai, I'm not mad at you. I'm sorry I was so grumpy."

"It's okay, Lila. I'm just glad we're okay," I said. "But I am sorry. I should have told you about the kiss right away. I don't want us to have any secrets. I was just so confused and angry that I didn't want to think about it."

"Because you hate him."

"Yes."

"Do you, though?" Lila asked, her voice gentle.

"Lila." I shot her a very stern look.

"He got you like the perfect gift, and you hate him for it?"

"That's not why I hate him," I said, frowning.

"I just wonder, Mai, why you're still so angry for what might have been a mistake. After all, he's been nothing but nice all summer, right?"

I blew out a breath. I didn't want to upset Lila. It was hard enough being apart. "I'll think about it, okay?"

She smiled. "That's all I'm saying. Now I have to get ready for band practice."

"And Alex." I waggled my eyebrows.

Lila blushed and lifted a pinkie to the screen. "Stay gold."

"Stay gold."

I successfully avoided Zach for the rest of the day. The next morning, I took my time getting ready. The twins had another single-day camp, and I didn't want to get roped into riding in the car with them because Zach was sure to ride along with them.

I had just changed out of my pajamas into a paisley-print dress when I heard feet stomping up the stairs. I braced myself as two pairs of tiny fists pounded on my closed door.

"Mai-nesan! Let us in!"

I opened the door and they charged inside, nearly knocking me backward.

"You never play with us anymore," Mason complained.

"*Never* is a strong word," I said, sitting on my bed as the Twin Tornados whirled around my room.

"What's that?" Ethan pointed to the framed magazine cover on the desk. Both boys walked right up to it and stuck their faces close to the glass.

"Are they your boyfriends?" Mason asked, sounding jealous. And adorable.

"No!" I laughed. "They're a music group I love."

Ethan's nose was almost touching the picture. "That boy looks like Zach."

I walked over to see who he was pointing at. Jungkook. My bias. "No way," I said, snatching the frame to protect it from greasy fingers. "They do not look anything alike!"

Mason jumped up and down. "That's the haircut Zach got right when school ended."

"What?" I looked at the picture again and squinted at it. Okay, there was a vague resemblance of hairstyle. Weird. "Do you want to hear their music?" I asked to distract the twins.

"Yes! Yes!" They leapt around my room.

Yikes! I put the frame on my nightstand out of their path of destruction. Then I opened my BTS playlist, hitting shuffle.

"YAY!" Ethan and Mason danced like kangaroos, bouncing and

bounding. They actually had pretty good rhythm. I joined them, spinning them around and laughing at all their silly moves.

Suddenly the opening strains of "Boy With Luv" started, and I lunged for my phone. But Mason grabbed my arms before I could forward past the song. "This is Zach's song!" he shouted.

"What are you talking about?" I asked.

"This is the song Zach listens to all the time," Ethan said.

"I don't think so," I said. They were obviously confused.

Then, to my utter shock and delight, Ethan and Mason executed perfectly timed shoulder lifts at the *oh yeah, oh yeah*s. I giggled and applauded.

Zach burst into my room and grabbed the boys. "There you are! Mom's been calling you both! You're going to be late for camp!"

"Zachy, we're doing your dance," Ethan said.

"What? Ha! No! Confused monsters!" Zach corralled the twins and herded them quickly out of my room, speaking to them in Japanese as they protested. Their voices faded, and then I heard the back door slam.

Well, that was just weird.

21

The weekend was a whirlwind of family activity: visiting the Mystic Seaport Museum, hiking at Barn Island, going to the beach, and our traditional jaunt to Watch Hill in Rhode Island to ride the merry-go-round, window-shop, and eat Del's frozen lemonade. Next Saturday was my birthday party, and then we'd fly home the following Saturday.

Usually I felt sad about leaving Mystic. This time, I was looking forward to getting away from Zach. I did feel a little sad, though. Things were changing. This summer in Mystic had made me realize that nothing stays the same. Wes was hardly around. Dad was on deadline. The twins had more energy than ever, but they were also more independent and happy to spend time with just each other.

And Zach. Zach was the most changed of everyone. He looked different. He dressed different. And his hair, now that the twins had pointed it out, had a decidedly K-pop vibe. Or maybe more like the Japanese bands he listened to.

He spoke Japanese. He wasn't afraid of spiders anymore. He wanted to travel the world. He was a completely different person from the one I thought I knew so well.

The only two people who seemed unchanged were Mom and Holly. They were as close as ever, pretty much joined at the hip since we arrived. They were the prime example of perfect BFF-dom. They were what Lila and I would be years from now.

I shifted on my bed and sighed. Even though I'd been hiding in my room ever since we got back from Watch Hill, I didn't want to be a hermit for the remaining two weeks I had in Mystic. Plus, I'd always loved celebrating my birthday. I didn't want the summer to end on a sour note, like it had two years ago. Besides, there would be presents. Who didn't love presents? I tried not to think about what Zach was getting me and how he'd told Noah and Celeste they had to be here to see it.

I sat up and stretched. Okay. Time to join the living. I would try to enjoy the rest of my summer here. Dad was sending off his graphic novel tomorrow, and he could finally relax. He'd even promised to go birding with me!

I ducked my head into the boys' room, wondering if the twins were there. Nope.

BZZZZZZZ! I patted my pocket, but the sound wasn't coming from my phone. I followed the buzzing to Zach's nightstand. His phone was charging . . . totally unattended! I glanced behind me, wondering where he was. Would I have time to get revenge after all? I quickly pulled my phone out and brought up the folder of Zach's embarrassing photos, with one ear cocked to the door in case Zach came upstairs.

I grinned in anticipation. I was finally going to get my revenge! But when I saw what was on Zach's screen, my grin disappeared. I wrinkled my nose in confusion.

It was an incoming text from Lila.

Lila Tan
It's done! I'm so excited!

For a brief second, I thought maybe I had the wrong phone and that Lila was texting me. I double-checked. No, this message from Lila was definitely on Zach's phone. Lila was texting Zach. Lila had Zach's phone number.

What did this mean?

I shook it off. I had my chance right now, right here. My heart pounded as I tapped on the photos in my folder, getting ready to AirDrop them onto Zach's phone. I fumbled Zach's passcode twice. Just as I was searching for his Instagram app, another text popped up.

Lila Tan
Mai is going to be so surprised and happy! Brilliant plan, Zach!

I squinted at her message. What was going on? What was I going to be happy about? I heard voices coming up the stairs. If I was going to post these pics to Zach's account, it had to be now.

But Lila's message flashed in my head. Surprised. Happy. Suddenly the thought of posting the pics didn't fill me with the same kind of glee as it had before. I mean, yes, I still wanted my revenge. I was still angry at Zach. But something else was mixing in with that anger. I dropped Zach's phone back onto his nightstand and made it back to my room, closing the door as the twins barreled into their room.

I quickly FaceTimed Lila, and she picked up immediately, grinning like she'd wanted me to call.

"Why are you texting Zach?" I asked sharply.

She looked immediately chastised. "Oh, Mai, it's not what you think."

"I don't know what to think. You said something about me being surprised and happy. What is going on?"

"It's nothing bad, I promise!"

I knew that! Lila was my best friend. I trusted her. But I did not trust Zach. "What are you two up to?"

"It's a surprise." Lila brought the screen close to her face, like she wanted to hug me. "I promise it's a good surprise. You'll understand soon, I swear! And I know you're going to love it!"

I must have made a face showing how I felt.

"Mai, I would never do anything to hurt you. You know that."

"I know," I said. But I couldn't say the same of Zach. I wish I could just let go. Moments ago, I'd had the perfect chance to get closure. With the press of a few buttons, I could have gotten my revenge so I could walk away from Zach. Forever.

But something bubbled in my chest. Pain? I shoved it down.

"How come you never get sad?" I blurted.

Lila's eyes widened in surprise. "I get sad."

"Not that I've ever seen."

"But you have. When I lost first chair. When my parents kept saying no to me forming a band. When I lost my favorite drumsticks and they made me save up to replace them."

"Yeah, but you were sad for like a second. I'm just saying, I wish I knew how to let disappointment go the way you do."

Lila was quiet, observing me while I squirmed. "I do feel sad sometimes," Lila said, "but I think of it kind of like a caterpillar."

"A what?"

"You know, they make a cocoon and then turn into a butterfly? I imagine I'm a caterpillar and let sadness wrap itself around me. But eventually I need to shed it and fly away. And when I do, I feel lighter. But even though I don't keep wearing my sad feelings, they're still a part of me because they make me who I become." Lila shook her head, her cheeks turning pink. "That probably sounds silly."

"No," I said, pondering. "That kind of makes sense."

We sat there, quietly, a little longer, Lila giving me time to process.

"I'm tired of feeling angry," I said finally. "I don't want to feel anything anymore. I wish I could just forget Zach, forget what he did, forget everything."

"I totally get why you're upset, Mai. What Zach did wasn't nice. But he had no idea you were there, listening. Maybe it was just easier for him to not say anything to those two guys."

"He should have defended me," I said.

"Sure. But we all make mistakes. And forgiving someone isn't the worst thing in the world," Lila said quietly.

"He laughed with those racist losers, Lila!"

"I know. But not everyone is like you."

"What's that supposed to mean?"

"You stand up for what you believe is right. You are amazing!

Those mean girls who gave me a hard time back in sixth grade scared me. I was never going to say anything to them. My plan was to avoid them and hope they'd eventually just get bored enough to leave me alone. But then you came along. You stepped in, spoke up, and told them off. You protected me."

"Best friends have each other's backs."

"Yes," Lila said. "But not everyone is as brave as you are. If the roles had been reversed, I'm not sure I could've done what you did for me. But I would have been there for you in other ways. I'd have walked you to your classes so you wouldn't have had to face them alone."

I nodded.

"And if I'd done that, Mai, would you hate me? If I hadn't stood up for you?"

"Of course not! I could never hate you!"

"You say that now, but look at how you feel about Zach for not defending you."

"That's different," I mumbled.

"How?"

I made a face, and Lila smiled the way she did whenever she knew she was right.

"I have to get ready for band practice," she said. "But I'll cancel it if you need me to."

"No," I said. "I'm fine. I'm better. Thanks, Lila. Stay gold."

I shoved my phone in my pocket, playing with the hem of my dress. Lila said I was brave, but she was wrong. I wasn't brave when it came to facing my feelings.

But maybe it was time to try to be.

22

I found Zach in the fort reading a travel book. He looked up when I entered, giving me a cautious smile. We hadn't spent any time alone together since Lila had arrived.

He put a bookmark in his book and set it down, then joined me at the table.

"We have to talk," I said.

"I know."

That surprised me. The next words he spoke surprised me even more.

"I'm sorry," he said, running his hand through his hair, ducking his chin like he used to when we were kids and he'd gotten in trouble.

Was he finally apologizing for what he'd done two years ago? Two easy words weren't going to cut it.

"That's not good enough," I said, my voice hard.

"I know, but I don't know what else to say. I hate that you're upset with me, but I get it. I mean, I thought we both wanted the same thing, but I shouldn't have assumed." Zach's sun-kissed cheeks flushed.

"Wait. What are you talking about?"

Our eyes connected, and my heart skipped a beat as I watched his lips form an answer. "The kiss."

Now it was my cheeks turning pink. "Oh. Right. The kiss."

"That's not why you're upset?" Zach asked. "You've been avoiding me ever since that day in town."

I mean, yeah, the kiss had taken me totally by surprise. But it didn't compare to what he'd done two years ago.

Zach interrupted my thoughts, his voice hopeful. "You're not mad that I kissed you?"

I shook my head, and then nodded, but then shook it again. I felt like one of those girls on TV who couldn't form coherent thoughts around a boy. That wasn't me. And Zach was no mere boy. This conversation about the kiss, like the actual kiss, just muddled everything that was important.

"I'm sorry," Zach said. "I mean, I'm not sorry I kissed you, but I am if it upset you." He sounded totally flustered. His hands fluttered in the air before he shoved them into his pockets.

I stared down at my own hands. Neither of us said anything for a long while, but it was far from silent. A chickadee scolded outside, and in the far-off distance a dog barked. And the blood rushing in my ears was so loud.

"I didn't come here to talk about that," I said.

"Okay," he said cautiously. "What do you want to talk about?"

Suddenly it all felt too hard. Coming here, facing Zach, talking about the past. I'd been so sure I could do this. Let go of the anger. But maybe that was impossible. I'd clung to it for so long.

I needed a reset button. "You're into Japanese rock now?"

Zach blinked at me. "Um. Yeah."

The silence drew out.

"That's what you wanted to talk about?" Zach looked understandably confused.

"Well, you shared your music with Lila." That sounded snotty. I tried to backtrack. "I mean, I always shared the music I loved with you."

"Right. Like BTS. And that song you loved. 'Boy With Luv.'" He smiled like everything was suddenly okay again.

The title of that song coming out of Zach's mouth felt like a slap.

"I do not love that song! Not anymore! Not since you ruined it for me!"

Now Zach looked like he'd been slapped.

"*I* ruined the song for you? How?" Zach blew out his breath in frustration. "You said you still stanned BTS!"

"I do! That has nothing to do with it!"

"Wasn't 'Boy With Luv' the song you danced to all summer two years ago?"

"Exactly!" I smacked my hand on the table. "*That* summer! That's the summer you ruined everything, Zachary Koyama!"

"I don't understand."

"You broke your own rule. You brought those guys to our fort. Our private fort where no one else was allowed."

"What guys?" And then understanding dawned. "Oh, those guys who were vacationing here? I forgot all about them."

Really? "Ryder and Colt."

"You remember their names." Zach seemed amused. Like he thought it was adorable.

"Don't even," I said with a snarl. "Those boys were the worst, but they weren't nearly as horrible as you."

Zach's head snapped back. "What do you mean?"

"I heard everything!"

Now Zach was starting to look angry. "Amai, I don't know what you're talking about! What did you hear? Did they say something to you?"

"Not to me! To you. About me!"

"But what does this have to do with the song?"

Oh my God! I took a deep breath. I needed to start from the beginning. So I did, listing each of his betrayals.

Betrayal 1: "You brought two strangers to our fort when you were the one to make the rule that no one but us was allowed in it."

Betrayal 2: "You let them watch quietly while I danced. I thought I was alone. It was a complete invasion of privacy."

Betrayal 3: "You totally abandoned me that week. You chose two boys you hardly knew and would never see again over the lifelong best friend you only got to see in the summer."

And then the ultimate unforgivable gigantic betrayal—

"I was going to get a treat from the bakery when I saw you and those two boys sitting outside," I said. All the heat from telling Zach about the first three betrayals left my voice. This was harder to share than I thought it would be. Talking about it meant remembering it, and I really didn't want to remember.

Zach remained quiet. He hadn't said one word. He seemed stunned.

"I was going to sneak up on you," I continued. "But when I got close enough, I heard what those boys were saying."

Zach's eyes got wide as he suddenly seemed to remember.

"Ryder made fun of my dancing. And you didn't say one thing to defend me. You're the one who said best friends looked out for each other, but you didn't stand up for me." A fresh wave of pain crashed into me. "Then they called the music 'ching-chong,' which, by the way, sounds nothing like Korean or any other language!"

Zach blinked.

"And do you remember what you did, Zach?" I didn't give him a chance to respond. "You laughed! You laughed with them about my dancing and you laughed at their racist garbage, like you not only agreed with them but thought it was funny for them to say terrible things about Asians. *You're* Asian, Zach!"

He finally looked ashamed. Good!

"I didn't agree with them!" he snapped.

"You didn't say *anything* about it! Silence is complicity!"

His face got bright red. "What about *your* silence? You held all this in for two years! Why didn't you say something to me?"

"Do not flip this back on me, Zachary Koyama! I thought you were my best friend!"

"Amai, I didn't know you were there. I didn't know you heard me."

"That shouldn't matter!" I shouted.

Zach crossed his arms, and his face turned stony and closed. And there it was. Zach hated having anyone point out he was wrong.

"You didn't even care that I stopped talking to you that last week of summer," I said. "You didn't even notice!"

Zach tightened his arms and frowned. "I noticed! You think I'm completely oblivious? Of course I noticed! And I cared! But I didn't know what was going on. I just thought you were nervous about starting middle school."

Clueless Zach!

"You should have said something," I said.

"Me? *You* should have said something! You're the one who was angry at me! We said we'd always tell each other how we felt! I didn't know you overheard me, Amai! And just for the record, I wasn't agreeing with anything those guys said. I didn't want to talk about anything with them."

"Then why did you spend all that time with them?"

"I don't know!"

"You win the prize for worst answer ever!" It was like an osprey had swooped down and plunged its talons deep into my heart, piercing it. "You always said we'd be loyal to each other. *You* said that! And I believed you." And then the tears came. "You told me I was your best friend. That you cared about me. But you lied! You never cared about me or our friendship at all!"

I bolted for the door and ran. Zach shouted my name. But it was the memory that chased me. I was fast but not fast enough to avoid it slamming into me. I made it to my room, but it was too late.

Who knew your heart could shatter a second time with the same pain?

TWO SUMMERS AGO

I was as still as a statue in the sweltering August heat, the back of my knees sticky with sweat as I remained crouched below the bakery patio wall. I wanted to bolt. How could Zach laugh? Ryder had insulted my dancing. Worse, he'd said something really racist. And Zach. Was. Laughing! I pressed my palms against the warm ground, ready to push off and run home.

"Dude," Ryder said, making me pause. "That girl has a huge crush on you."

"Who? Amai?" Zach said. "No!"

I frowned.

"Yeah. I can totally tell by the way she looks at you, like she has heart eyes." Ryder laughed. "Zach's got a girlfriend!"

"No! That's gross!" Zach made a gagging sound.

"You loooove her," Ryder sang.

"No way, dude! I could never!"

I felt like I'd been punched in the stomach. I must have looked sick because a lady came over to me and asked if I was okay.

No. I was not okay, but I nodded to her even as my tears started to fall. The pain had moved up from my stomach. My pulverized heart turned to dust. Wiping my eyes, I pushed my way through the crowd to the bookstore to wait for Dad and tried to get a grip on myself.

I held back my tears in the car, but when Dad pulled up into the driveway, I ran to my room, blasted my music, and cried. I'd left my broken heart back at the bakery, and yet I could feel it pounding in my chest.

All the summers Zach and I had spent making memories together, sharing secrets, having adventures, watching movies, hiking on trails, whispering at night, laughing, talking—they meant everything to me. But now I knew they meant nothing to Zach. No wonder he'd rather hang around with those boys. No wonder he didn't defend me. He never had my back, and he never would.

I successfully stayed away from Zach all week, but it was nearly impossible to avoid him at my birthday party. When the families gathered at the table for lunch, Zach managed to sit next to me, even though I was at the head of the table with Ethan and Mason on either side of me. The chair screeched as he dragged it and shoved it next to mine. I ate like my food was the most fascinating thing ever, staring at my plate and chewing with great focus.

After the dishes were cleared, Zach rummaged in a bag next to his feet.

"Happy birthday, Amai!" he shouted, placing the cake party hat that he'd worn on his birthday at the start of summer onto my head.

I frowned and knocked it off. When it fell to the floor, the twins scrambled for it, arguing over who got to wear it. Zach leaned forward to peer at my face.

"Before we have cake, I have something to share," Wes said, standing up at the table.

I was grateful for the interruption. For some reason, Zach reached for my hand. I yanked my arm away so quickly that I bumped my elbow hard against the arm of my chair and gasped.

"Amai!" Zach exclaimed. "Are you hurt?"

Before I could tell him exactly how hurt I was, Wes announced that he had taken a two-year assignment in Japan. The Koyamas were moving to Tokyo next month.

I sprang from the table, announcing I had to use the bathroom. I stayed there for a long time. Long enough for Mom to come find me.

"Mai," she said, knocking on the door. "Are you feeling okay?"

I wiped the tears from my face and opened the door. I wanted to tell her what Zach had done.

"Oh, sweetie." Mom leaned against the wall, looking down at me with a sad smile. "I know. I feel the same way. We are going to miss them tremendously, but they will be back! Come on. Put on a happy face for them. This is good news for Wes."

So I did what Mom asked. I forced myself to smile for the rest of my party, but I would not talk to Zach. Not then and not ever again.

Worst birthday ever.

23

That memory reminded me that nothing had changed. Zach had zero remorse for what he'd done. I'd tried talking to Zach like Lila had wanted, but now everything was worse.

Mom believed me when I told her I was really tired from the full day and excused me from dinner, yet even though I insisted I wasn't hungry, she brought up a turkey sandwich and a bowl of fresh raspberries from the Koyama garden anyway.

I tried to listen to music—it usually cheered me up, but tonight nothing could make me feel better. When I replayed the argument with Zach, I broke down all over again, crying like he'd betrayed me only yesterday. My pillow was soaked in an ocean of tears.

I was so tired of crying and so tired of feeling badly. All I could do was change into my pj's, crank up the AC, and go to bed. Crying had exhausted me, and I fell into a deep sleep.

I dreamed that I was on the pond in Zach's canoe. I knew I'd be in trouble for going out by myself. Paddling was hard—no matter how strongly I pulled, the boat wouldn't move forward. Yet somehow, I was so far away from shore that I couldn't see the house anymore. Anxiety fluttered in my stomach. How was I going to get home? I sliced the paddle in the water and pulled with every ounce of strength I had, but nothing happened. The canoe stayed completely still.

"Help!" I wanted to shout into the fog rolling in across the pond's surface, but my voice wouldn't work.

I couldn't get home. I was adrift and alone.

A gunshot echoed in the air, and I jerked awake. My sheets tangled around my arms, and I blinked against the brightness of my room.

"She's still sleeping!" Mason called, running back down the stairs.

Well, now I'm not.

The gunshot from my dream had only been Mason slamming my bedroom door. I looked at the time on my phone and groaned. It was 11:00 a.m. How had I slept so long? And how was it that all I wanted to do was go back to sleep?

A light knock pulled me from my thoughts.

"Go away," I said, pulling the covers over my head. I wasn't in the mood for the Twin Tornados.

"Mai?"

I yanked the covers down. It was Mom. "Come in," I said.

She walked in and placed a mug of hot chocolate on my night-stand. Mom wasn't a fan of air conditioners, so she turned the dial down a notch. Then she leaned over and touched the back of her hand to my forehead. "Are you feeling okay?" she asked.

"I'm fine." I sat up and sipped the hot chocolate. "Mmm. This is good. Thanks."

Mom sat down on my bed. "Did something happen between you and Zach?"

I shook my head, making my eyes wide and innocent.

"He's being very quiet," Mom said. "Holly said he hasn't said one word since yesterday. And it's not like you to skip dinner."

I was not in the mood for an enforced Peace Talk and took another sip from my mug even though I wasn't really thirsty. "Everything's fine, Mom."

Instead of taking the hint and leaving as I'd hoped, Mom smoothed my comforter but wouldn't meet my eyes. "Friendships can be tricky, sometimes," she said. "Especially ones that have lasted a long time."

I so did not want a lecture about how I needed to be nice to Zach or whatever. Mom and Holly had a perfect friendship. Zach and I did not.

"And when you spend a lot of time apart, that can also make things challenging."

Oh my God. Why was Mom talking to me about this? There was nothing she could do or say to make things better between me and Zach.

"Are you and Zach fighting over anything specific, or has it just been hard to reconnect?"

I set my mug on my nightstand and drew my knees up to my chest. "I told you, Mom, everything's fine."

She smiled at me, but her eyes were full of concern. Reaching over, she brushed a lock of hair out of my eyes. "Holly and I have worked very hard to stay connected over the years," Mom said, dropping her hand back into her lap. "But there was a time during college when we stopped speaking to each other."

That got my attention. "You did?"

Mom nodded. "We didn't talk for almost two years."

"But why?"

"We had a falling-out. A disagreement. At the time, it felt very huge and important. But when I look back on it now, it was all misunderstandings and hurt feelings. If it wasn't for Holly reaching out, well, who knows what might have happened. I can be pretty stubborn."

"I can't believe that you and Holly stopped talking," I said. "I mean, you two are like the perfect friends."

Mom shrugged. "Like I said, we work at it. We talk to each other about how we feel. We say something when we're feeling slighted. Sometimes we need to apologize. All relationships have their ups and downs."

I was still grappling with the shock of Mom and Holly having had a falling-out when Mom dropped another bomb. "We had words two years ago. I was upset that she and Wes were moving to Japan and that Holly hadn't discussed it with me."

"Yeah!" That was exactly how I'd felt, too. I never thought about how Mom might have taken the news.

"I was shocked," Mom said. "So I took Holly aside and basically berated her for keeping that a secret. Holly felt horrible, of course. She had wanted to tell me, to talk it over with me, but Wes wanted it to be a family decision. And then he was just so excited and proud of his promotion that he insisted Holly keep it a secret so that he could share the news himself. She couldn't say no."

I frowned. Holly should have told Mom! Best friends didn't keep big secrets like that.

Mom caught my frown and patted my leg. "I was really hurt, but when I thought about it, I would have done the same for your dad. And if I'd promised something to Dad, I'd keep it."

Then Holly shouldn't have promised. She should have known it would upset Mom. And Zach should have told me. Though I guess since I'd already learned he and I weren't best friends, it hadn't mattered that he hadn't said anything to me.

"But," Mom went on, "it really was a great opportunity for them. And I don't blame them at all for taking it. And while I was upset that Holly hadn't confided in me, I eventually understood. Just because we're best friends, she doesn't owe me. That's not how friendship works. But it was a shock when they announced it for sure."

"Are you still upset?" I asked.

Mom smiled. "Of course not. In fact, we made up later that afternoon. We'd already stopped talking for two years in college, and neither of us wanted to repeat that. Our friendship means too much. We do the work, Mai. We apologize and we forgive because that's what friends do."

"But what if one friend does something truly unforgivable?"

Mom cocked her head at me. She looked at me for so long that I squirmed under her scrutiny.

"I guess it depends. Do you want to talk to me about it?"

No way. It was too humiliating. Too painful. I shook my head.

Mom looked surprised and hurt. "You don't like talking to me about what's going on with you, I know. I suppose it's natural at your age, but I do want you to know I'm here."

"But only for good things," I said, squeezing my pillow.

"What do you mean?"

"You only want to hear when I'm happy."

"What? No, Mai, that's not true. Why would you think that?"

"Because when I'm sad, you always want me to snap right out of it." I patted my pillow.

"Well, of course I don't like it when you're sad, but that doesn't mean I don't want you to be able to talk about it with me."

"Remember when I was in the third grade and Becca disinvited me from her birthday party? I wanted to talk to you, but you were on a video conference in the kitchen. I stood there, waiting for you to be done."

Mom nodded. "Yes, and when I saw you with tears in your eyes, I stepped away."

"And then when I told you why I was crying, you got mad at me."

Mom froze, her eyes running back and forth like she was watching a movie. Then her face went slack. "Oh, Mai. I remember now. It was my first meeting that I was running, and my boss was on the call. I was already stressed out about it. But you always come first. I didn't mind having to step away—I guess I just thought you had been injured or something. I'm sorry. That was a lousy way for me to have reacted."

I blinked. "You always tell me not to be sad, anytime I might even look sad. Even after Wes's announcement, you said you were sad, but you told me to act happy."

Mom stared at me. "Oh my goodness. And that's why you don't tell me when you're feeling sad?"

"It's why I *don't* feel sad." I realized something. I pushed sadness away and let anger replace it. Anger was an easier emotion to deal with. It gave me purpose instead of just . . . emptiness. But if that was true, then I wasn't angry at Zach. I was sad. Because he had hurt my feelings.

Mom wrapped me in a tight hug. "I'm sorry. That's not what I intended at all." She pulled back, holding my shoulders and looking at me. "See? Even mother-daughter relationships take work. I mess up, I apologize, and hopefully you forgive me. I'm sorry, Mai. I'll be better about listening when you're feeling sad or angry or happy or, well, anything. Can you forgive me?"

I nodded.

"Are you sure you don't want to talk to me about anything else?"

I shook my head. I wasn't trying to punish Mom, but after years of keeping my feelings in, it was going to take time to be able to talk about them.

"Okay." Mom stood. "Come downstairs, and be a part of the family again. Zach seems pretty down, not that it's your job to make him happy. But I think the two of you should at least talk."

We *had* talked. And things were worse than ever.

Mom left my room, and I thought about everything she'd said. That friendships took work.

Lila had told me I was brave.

Celeste said it was better to forgive.

So that was it. I had to make a choice. I had to either forgive Zach or let him go forever.

24

There were four days left until my party, seven until my actual birthday, when we'd go to the zoo in Rhode Island, and eleven until we flew home. Eleven days to decide whether or not I could forgive Zach.

I made it to the porch just as everyone was finishing breakfast. Dad looked like himself again, no more bags under his eyes, no more worry lines on his forehead.

The twins hugged me hello and goodbye, then ran off to their tree house.

Mom gave me a meaningful look. I sighed.

"Where's Zach?" I asked.

"He went for a bike ride," Holly said. "I told him to wait for you."

I shook my head. "No, it's okay."

We talked about the menu for my birthday party. I was happy that Holly was doing the cooking. She'd always loved to try out new recipes, but living in Tokyo had made a big difference. Mom liked playing sous chef. I secretly hoped she was picking up tips to bring home.

I watched Mom and Holly like they were two rare species of birds, observing every nuance. They seemed the same as always, laughing and talking and acting as close as two people could be. If Mom hadn't told me she'd gotten upset with Holly about her decision to move to Japan, I'd have never guessed. Maybe what Mom and Holly had was just special and rare.

I went to the fort, glad to know that Zach wouldn't be there. As I sat down with my binoculars, I realized I'd forgotten to call Margie. I pulled out her business card, punched her number into my phone, then hit the call button. Old people preferred talking on the phone to texting, plus I really wanted to hear her reaction.

Just as Margie picked up the phone, Zach walked into the fort. My heart leapt in my throat. He hesitated for a second, but when he saw I was on the phone, he nodded and went to sit in his chair with a book.

"Mystic Nature Center and Camp. This is Margie."

"Hi, Margie! This is Mai, from the house on Egret Pond?"

"Hello, Mai. It's nice to hear from you. Do you have news for me?"

"I do! I saw the barn owl!"

"That's wonderful! Tell me everything."

I rattled off the details of seeing the barn owl last week, keenly aware that I was no longer alone.

"What a lucky young lady you are to have had such a truly magical experience," Margie said when I was done. "Thanks for letting me know."

"I haven't seen the owl since then, though."

"That doesn't mean it isn't around. Maybe you'll see it again."

"I hope so!" But I hadn't been back out in the woods in days. So much had happened that I hadn't had time to think about birding. The summer was floating away.

"You saw the barn owl?" Zach sat down next to me on the bench as I ended the call, close but not too close.

I swallowed. I hadn't decided yet what to do about Zach. My anger felt less like a flame and more like a fizzled-out match. And to be honest, I was exhausted. It was tiring carrying around all that anger. But that was not a good enough reason to forgive, and it was certainly not enough to make me forget.

But Celeste and Noah would be here in four days for my birthday party. And with everyone around, and Mom and Holly at least somewhat aware that something was up between me and Zach, I had to either work things out or just accept that we were going to be awkward. And there was the matter of the birthday surprise that Zach and Lila were planning.

"Amai?"

I'd been silent too long. I took a breath. "Yeah. You heard

me talking to Margie. I saw the barn owl last week."

"That's great," Zach said quietly.

I fiddled with the straps of the binoculars.

Zach cleared his throat, and I tensed. "Hey, Amai?"

"What?"

"Can we talk about what happened?"

"No."

"I can't stand that I hurt you."

"It's fine. I'm over it."

"Are you, though?"

I glanced at him, his face so full of concern. "I am." Okay, so that was a lie, but I was working hard to make it the truth. "Can we just move on?"

"I don't know." Zach crossed his arms so tightly he was hugging himself.

"Let's just call a truce, okay?" There. Done. Eleven more days. I just had to be okay for eleven more days. Maybe I didn't have to decide if I could forgive Zach. Maybe we could just pretend everything was fine. Fool our families. Fool ourselves.

"I don't like this," Zach said. "It feels like we're not friends anymore."

I shook my head.

"I messed up," Zach said. "I know I did. I'm sorry."

I stood up. "Okay. Fine."

"Fine?"

I knew Zach didn't want to talk about this any more than I did. "Yes, fine."

In the distance, I could hear Mason calling me.

To prove to Zach—and myself—that I could do this, I said, "I promised Mason a picnic in the backyard. You want to join us?"

I could see the confusion on Zach's face, but I ignored it. He could join us or not, but one thing was for sure, I wasn't ready to forgive him. And I probably never would be.

But we could at least act like we were okay. We'd done it earlier this summer, and we could do it now. So Zach and I made sandwiches for lunch, with Mason and Ethan "helping," had our picnic, and watched a movie with the twins. When they left to take their naps, I was all set with an excuse to escape.

"I need to figure out what to wear for the party." Not that I was into dressing up like Zach liked to these days. I just had to get away from him. I'd been acting all summer, pretending to feel things I didn't. It was confusing and tiring.

Zach put the TV remote on the coffee table and turned to me. "Can we just talk about that summer? Can I just explain what was going on?"

"You don't need to explain it, Zach. I was there. I heard you!"

Zach leaned his head back, a little too hard. "How many times do I have to apologize, Amai? What do I have to do to prove I'm sorry?"

"Nothing," I tossed over my shoulder as I headed for the stairs. "There's nothing you can do." Not unless he could go back in time and prove he cared about our friendship two summers ago.

When I got to my bedroom, I went straight to my closet. Mom always took a billion photos on my birthday. I might as well look good. This might be the last summer I spent in Mystic. I wasn't sure how, but I was going to convince my parents to let me skip next summer. Maybe I could stay with Lila. Or Dad could stay home with me. He'd probably have to work anyway.

I yanked on the chain to turn on the closet light. But I'd forgotten that the brass bird pull was persnickety and needed to be tugged gently. The bird unhooked and fell, tumbling into the far corner of the closet where the ceiling sloped down to meet the wood-planked floor.

I sighed and got down on my hands and knees to retrieve it. As I scooped it up, something glinted from the floor. I leaned closer and glimpsed something silver.

It was the little rabbit charm Zach had given me. The one I had torn off my wrist and flung into the closet two summers ago. I held it in my palm, stroking it. My heart twisted at the memory of callously throwing this bunny away, and the tiny, lonesome sound it had made when it had hit the wall.

"I'm sorry for abandoning you," I whispered.

I knew it was stupid to feel bad for an inanimate object, but I couldn't help it. I'd thrown the little guy away even though he'd meant the world to me.

And as the minutes ticked by, I realized that it wasn't really the charm I felt bad for.

TWO SUMMERS AGO

The morning of my eleventh birthday, instead of feeling excited like I had for every birthday before, I was annoyed. I wished we could just skip it and go home to Sunnyvale.

Zach kept trying to talk to me all week, but I ignored him. How could he pretend to still be friends when he'd refused to defend me?

I slid out of bed, careful not to hit my head on the ceiling. As I padded to the closet to grab some clothes, I noticed something under my door. A white envelope. I flipped it over and when I saw my name in Zach's printing, my heart did a little skip and I almost smiled. I almost felt happy.

But then I remembered how he'd failed me. There was nothing he could say in a birthday card that would make up for it. Even if he apologized, it wouldn't be enough. All our lives he'd pledged his loyalty to me, to our friendship, but he was a liar. Actions spoke louder than words, and his actions destroyed any good feelings I ever had for him. I crumpled the envelope as best as I could, and I threw it in the back of my closet. It could rot there forever with his stupid rabbit charm.

25

The memory surprised me. I had completely forgotten about the card. I shoved the rabbit charm into my pocket and crawled to the back of the closet, patting my hand around on the floor. There in the far back corner covered in dust bunnies was the crumpled envelope. I clutched it as I backed out of the closet and sat down on my bed.

Placing the envelope on my lap, I smoothed it out and traced my finger over the letters of my name. Amai might have been the name given to me by my parents, but Zach was the only one who called me that. And it had always felt special.

Whatever this card said couldn't make things worse than they already were. I was curious, though, and took a deep breath for courage.

Before I could talk myself out of it, I pulled out a card. On the front was an ink drawing of a rabbit wearing a birthday hat. The words *It's some bunny special's birthday* made me smile despite myself.

It took another deep breath to steady my jangly nerves so I could start reading.

Happy 11th birthday, Amai! I hope you get everything you want and more because you always deserve the best.

I know you're nervous about starting middle school. (I can tell by the way you've been a little grumpy this week.) But you are smart and brave and kind. You'll be fine!

I'm glad we're best friends. And because we are, I'd never keep a secret from you, so here it goes. We're moving to Japan for two years for my dad's job. I don't want to go. I guess it's a good opportunity (as Mom says). Anyway, best friends don't keep secrets. This isn't the best news for your birthday, but I didn't want you to be surprised when Dad announces it later. And I promise we'll be back. Maybe we can write to each other while I'm in Japan? That would be fun. Old-fashioned letters like this card! What do you think?

Happy birthday to my best friend forever.

♥ Zach

I read Zach's note twice. And then a third time. He'd told me about moving to Tokyo after all, and if I'd read the card instead of throwing it away, I wouldn't have been shocked by Wes's announcement. Words. They were just words, but these words from Zach meant a lot. Had I read this two summers ago, I might have been able to reexamine my anger and hurt. Maybe I would have been able to talk to him about what I'd overheard. And maybe I wouldn't have spent the last two years hating him. Maybe.

But actions spoke louder than words. And when I reflected on Zach's actions this summer, I felt the warm flush of shame creep up my neck. His thoughtful gifts from Japan, the way he kept trying to reconnect with me or stubbornly ignored my rudeness. He wasn't pretending to be nice. He wasn't acting or lying. That was me. So who was the faker here?

Lila was wrong—I wasn't a brave person. Maybe the hard truth was that I was a judgmental coward. I was starting to realize that I didn't want to lose Zach. His friendship was important to me. It was why I'd been so angry and hurt that he'd thrown it away in the first place. But he hadn't. This card was proof.

Deep down, I knew I needed to forgive Zach. I wanted to forgive him. But I wasn't sure if it was too late to fix what had broken between us.

By the morning of my birthday party, I still hadn't found the courage to talk to him.

Dad had taken the twins to pick up my gelato cake. Wes was putting up the big canopy on the lawn while Zach dragged out the tables and chairs from the basement. Mom and Holly had been cooking since dawn. The smell of karaage, my favorite Japanese-style fried chicken, drifted out onto the back porch where I was sitting, pretending to read my bird book.

Zach wore pastel green shorts with a white polo shirt, collar flipped up in the back, and white socks with white kicks. He was dressed up but still looked vaguely like summer Zach in shorts, though these were nicer than his old baggy cargos.

I was slightly embarrassed that he and I looked like we'd inadvertently coordinated our outfits. I'd been wearing dresses most of the summer and wanted to look a little different for my thirteenth birthday party, so I'd put on bright pink shorts that kind of looked like a miniskirt, a mint-green short-sleeve hoodie, retro white knee socks with pink stripes, and white sneakers.

Every time Zach passed on his way to the basement or back out to the lawn with a few more chairs under his arms, he flashed me a grin. I smiled back but also felt guilty. I'd told him everything was okay, but it hadn't been the truth. I had unloaded all my anger on him but hadn't given him the chance to respond. Not really. If I truly believed that friendship was about loyalty and honesty, I needed to change that. To talk to him before everyone got here, before I opened whatever gift he and Lila got for me. Otherwise I might end up feeling more guilty than happy. And I wanted to feel happy again more than anything.

As I watched Zach set up the last two chairs, I patted my pocket—where I'd stashed his birthday card from two years ago—and left the safety of the porch.

"Hey," I called out to him.

Zach straightened and turned to face me. He smiled again, but it didn't reach his eyes. He was acting the way he thought I wanted him to. And maybe that was the problem. I'd been playing the part of a fake best friend all summer long, and now Zach was realizing it. I just didn't know how to get us back to where we were before. Maybe that was impossible. Maybe what we had really was gone forever.

"I need to talk to you," I said.

Zach gave me his full attention, his brown eyes sharp, like a hawk's.

I fiddled with my pocket. "I know I said things between us were okay, but—"

"They're not?" Zach sounded hurt.

"No! I mean yes. We're okay, but I wasn't being completely honest with you."

"About what?"

"It's complicated. I found this . . ." I pulled out the card to show him, just as an unfamiliar car pulled into the driveway. Noah and Celeste piled out, and when Celeste saw me, she broke into a run and threw her arms around me, squeezing my breath out. She let go with a grin and shouted, "Happy birthday, Mai!"

"Thanks."

Noah put a wrapped gift in my arms. "Happy birthday. Thanks for having us."

"Thanks for coming." I shook the box.

"Hey! No guessing!" Celeste laughed and snagged the gift back from me. She ran over to place it on a table piled with gifts from my parents and Zach's. I was glad that Celeste and I were good. My brain had been so focused on old friendships this summer that I hadn't really had a chance to appreciate the new ones. And Celeste was definitely a friend.

Which meant I'd have to wait till later to talk to Zach. As I shoved the envelope back in my pocket, I saw Zach watching, his mouth open. Noah wrapped his arm around Zach's neck in a combination hug and headlock, and the moment was over.

Noah's mom's car pulled out, and seconds later, Dad pulled up.

Mason leapt out of the car. "Happy birthday, Mai-nesan!"

"Me first!" shouted Ethan, catching up quickly.

They both tackled me in a dual hug, making me laugh. Mom and

Holly brought out lunch while Wes wrangled the boys into sitting down at the table. Celeste grabbed my arm and pulled me over so I could sit with her on one side and Zach on the other. Holly had outdone herself—the food was amazing. Karaage, gyoza, potato salad, chirashizushi, inarizushi. All my favorite Japanese homemade foods. Celeste was her curious self, asking about the food, trying everything, and loving it all. Zach and Noah talked nonstop about some online game they'd been playing all week. Every so often, I'd feel Zach's gaze on me. I turned to catch his eyes, a question in them, and tried to answer with a reassuring smile. If only we hadn't been interrupted earlier. I vowed to make it right after the party when I could talk with him alone.

"Presents or cake?" Holly asked me after lunch.

"Cake!" Ethan shouted.

"Presents!" Mason yelled.

"Now, boys, you know the rule," Wes said.

"Let's do cake," I said, even though I was pretty full. Nerves made the choice for me. Lila had mentioned some secret surprise she and Zach had cooked up, and suddenly I wasn't sure I wanted to know what it was.

Celeste and Noah fell into a deep conversation about the upcoming school semester. Apparently they only had one class together. This was my chance to talk to Zach.

I turned, but he wasn't sitting beside me anymore. Before I could go looking for him, Wes came back outside. Instead of cake, he was carrying his laptop and the wireless speakers from the house.

"A little treat before the treat," he said, smiling.

Dad helped the moms clear off the table as Wes set the laptop in front of me. Zach reappeared and leaned over me to click on a file, his hair brushing against my cheek. It smelled like coconut.

Zach hit play and stepped away, and my eyes grew wide as I recognized the person in the video.

26

"Hey, Mai, happy birthday!" Lila sat at her drum kit. "I composed this for your birthday."

She gazed at the camera with her serious drummer girl expression, then started a beat on the bass, her knee bouncing as she tapped the pedal. She smacked the cymbals with a metallic crash, and her sticks danced over the drums, making me nod my head along with the beat. The rhythmic thumps vibrated against my ribs. After a couple of minutes, she switched to what I knew was a drum fill, and I smiled as I watched the pure joy on her face. As she returned to the main groove, I realized I could listen to her forever. Finally she spun her sticks as the thudding beat of the bass pounded, and she hammered her way into a glorious finale.

I cheered even though she couldn't hear me. Everyone around

me also clapped and whooped. It was then that I realized that Celeste was holding Zach's phone up.

She smiled and handed it to me. There was Lila on FaceTime.

"AHHHH," I shouted. "That was amazing!"

She grinned. "Thank you! So much fun! And it was great seeing you watch the video. Happy birthday, Mai!"

"I can't believe you did this! You've gotten so good, Lila. The Hot Pinx are going to totally slay the talent show, and . . ." I trailed off because of a commotion going on behind me.

"Hey, Mai?" Lila said quickly, recapturing my attention.

"Hmm?"

"This was my gift to you, but Zach's is coming next."

"Oh?"

"Hand this phone back to Celeste and then turn around."

I did as she said. When I swiveled in my chair, I was surprised to find Zach standing in the walkway with his back to me. He had put on a long white linen shirt, which hung down like a coat.

Suddenly the very familiar opening notes from "Boy With Luv" blasted from the speakers, and before I could react, Zach started doing the choreography from the BTS video. My mouth dropped open. Out of the corner of my eye, I could see Noah holding up his phone to record my reaction and then turning the phone back to Zach. But I couldn't take my eyes off Zach as he moved his shoulders, dancing Jimin's part. I shouted along with everyone else. Zach was good. He was really good!

At the start of the chorus, though, he locked eyes with me and crooked a finger without missing a step of the dance. I blinked. No way could I join him. I hadn't done this routine in two years.

But Celeste nudged me and I could hear Lila shouting from the phone, her voice tinny and far away, "Go, Mai! Go, Mai! Go, Mai!"

I couldn't resist. I jumped up and joined Zach, dancing Jungkook's part as I used to. By the end of the chorus, Zach and I were in perfect sync, the moves automatically coming back to me. I couldn't stop grinning and didn't think I could get any happier. But then on the last chorus, Mason and Ethan jumped in, and the four of us finished the dance with our families and friends cheering us on.

As the last note faded, I fought to catch my breath. Zach shot me a mischievous grin and raised his eyebrows at me. I threw myself into his arms as Mason and Ethan hugged on to our legs.

After lots of laughter and high fives and compliments, I grabbed Zach's phone from Celeste for a minute of one-on-one time with my BFF.

"Thank you, Lila. That was the best birthday surprise ever."

"You should really thank Zach," she replied. "All of it, even my drum solo, was his idea."

We said our goodbyes, my heart still pumping long after the

cardio had ended. It kept up a steady rhythm through the birthday song, the delicious cake (not that I really noticed what it tasted like), and the gift opening.

Noah, Celeste, Zach, and I played three rounds of cornhole, and it felt like I was observing myself from afar. I couldn't stay in the moment—my mind was too busy replaying Zach's dance . . . and me dancing with him.

It was late in the afternoon when Mrs. Murdocca came to pick up Noah and Celeste. I gave Celeste a big hug and promised to keep in touch. Just before she got in the car, she whispered, "Don't break his heart."

As everyone else cleaned up, I went to lie down in Mom's hammock. Above the branches of the apple tree, the clouds drifted across a wide blue summer sky.

"Hey," Zach said, appearing next to me.

I smiled up at him. "Hey." Suddenly I felt shy. Something I'd never ever felt around him before. "That was really amazing. Thank you. And don't tell Lila, but *it* was the best gift ever." Though I knew she'd agree.

"Can I join you?" he asked.

And like we had when we were younger, we shared the hammock. We were bigger and heavier, so we sloped toward each other in the middle, our shoulders and legs pressing together.

I wasn't sure where to begin. "Zach, I—"

"Let me talk, okay, Amai?" he interrupted.

I nodded as we both stared up at the sky.

"I'm sorry," he said. "I'm sorry I didn't have your back when those guys said such evil things. I'm sorry for acting like I didn't care about you. I lied when I told Ryder I didn't like you. But I didn't like the way he was talking about you. And I just wanted him to stop, so I changed the subject. How I went about it was wrong, and I'm sorry."

Zach took a deep breath, and I felt him look at me.

"I knew you were upset about something that last week, but I seriously never thought it was that. I had no clue you'd heard us. I know that isn't an excuse. I should have been better."

We were quiet for a while, my pounding heart the only sound as I contemplated what to say. But Zach spoke first.

"Is that the card I wrote to you for your birthday that summer?"

I pulled it out of my pocket. "Yeah."

"Why didn't you say anything about it? I mean, I figured you were really upset we were moving, but it would have been nice if we could have talked about it. And written letters. I really missed you. And when that first summer rolled around and we weren't here in Mystic—we weren't together—I realized how much you mean to me. I kept waiting for you to write."

I felt my face get warm. "I didn't read your card."

The hammock swayed as Zach leaned toward me. "What do you mean?"

"I mean, I was still mad about what I'd heard you say, so I tossed it in the closet. I only found it and read it last week."

We swayed in the hammock for a few moments longer. Somehow it was easier to talk this way, side by side, instead of facing each other.

"I'm sorry, too, Zach. I should have talked to you right away, or at least before our summer ended. I was just so sad, and I let that sadness turn into anger because it was easier to deal with. I thought I didn't want us to be friends anymore, but that's not true. You're my very best friend."

I felt the hammock shift. Zach's face loomed over mine. "Same. I thought of you the whole time I was in Japan, which is why I couldn't stop collecting gifts for you. Everything reminded me of you, and I wished you were there with me."

I smiled up at him. "We only have a week left before I go home. Let's make the most of it. I forgive you, Zach. Do you forgive me?"

"I do, Amai." He looked down at me and cleared his throat. "But I don't want to be just friends. Maybe we can be . . . more?"

"What . . . ? I mean . . . are you . . . ? Yes . . ." My words got tangled in my mouth as our eyes locked. Zach smiled at me.

"Hey! Let me up!" Ethan launched himself onto the hammock, making it swing dangerously.

Zach laughed and wrapped an arm around me protectively.

"I want on, too!" Mason tugged on the hammock and tipped it, making all of us tumble to the grass. We laughed like it was the funniest thing that had ever happened.

Like the ugly memories that had been hanging over us had blown away with the breeze.

Like summer would never end.

My heart was full.

AMAZUPPAI: SWEET AND SOUR

THE LAST WEEK OF SUMMER

Sweet

Cottony clouds reflected in the surface of the water, which shimmered as the ripples from our paddles moved together in a perfectly choreographed rhythm, and we glided across the pond like a pair of swans. Zach smoothly turned the canoe as we approached the birch trees.

I'd added three new birds to my list in the past two days, although we hadn't seen the osprey. But I hadn't given up hope. One thing I'd learned this summer was that there was always hope for wishes to come true.

Zach and I hadn't spoken one word during this trip on the pond. The only sounds were birdsong blending with the plops of water dripping off our paddles as we made our way back to shore. But it was the best kind of silence, the kind that is full of unspoken things and good feelings and a deep connection—to nature and to each other.

At the stone steps, Zach disembarked and then held the canoe steady, taking my hand to help me out, as he had the last two days. But this time he didn't drop it as we walked back toward the house. And I didn't pull it out of his grasp.

Sweet

Margie gave me and Zach a personal guided tour of the Mystic Nature Center. She even took us into the hospital where an osprey that someone had rescued was resting. It had gotten tangled in some weeds, but Margie said it would recover with a little time and care.

The best part was getting to go along with her when she released the osprey back into the wild. We watched in awed silence as the bird flapped its wings and lifted off from the ground, soaring higher and higher into the air until it disappeared beyond the trees on the other side of the river.

Maybe I would have a job like Margie's when I grew up. Study wildlife or birds. The possibilities seemed endless.

Sour

The day before I went home, I folded my clothes and packed them into my suitcase so slowly, Mom had to ask me to get a move on three times. I wasn't ready to leave. I wanted to do our whole summer over again.

"Hey."

I turned from my suitcase to see Zach at my door and smiled. "Hey."

He raised his eyes in question, and I nodded, inviting Zach into my room.

"This is definitely coming home with me," I said, pointing to the framed magazine cover he'd given me.

Zach smirked. "Should I be jealous?"

I was going to make a joke, then realized I didn't want to make light of anything he said. Not now. I shook my head. "No."

Zach sat down on the bed, next to my open suitcase.

"I wish I'd talked to you at the start of summer," I said. "I feel like we wasted time."

Zach looked up at me with those warm brown eyes that made my heart do fluttery things in my chest.

"I'm sorry," I said, my throat closing, a warning that tears would be following.

"Me too, Amai." Zach took my hand and squeezed gently. "But we're okay now."

A promise. One that I wanted to believe. I'd once discounted Zach's promise, and that led to nothing but heartache. What if being apart changed things again? What if when I came back here next summer Zach changed? What if I changed? And what if our feelings changed? My hand clasped in his gave me hope, but a part of me was also scared.

Sweet

Our last day was one of traditions. Mom and Holly always spent our final hours in their hammocks. They said it was too hard to say goodbye at the airport, so Wes was always the only one to drive us. Zach and I chose to get in one more quality hang at the fort.

"Last present," Zach said.

"What? I thought you gave me all my gifts already?" And truly, what could top the dance at my birthday party? I'd downloaded

Noah's recording and already watched it a million times.

"This is something I picked up last week." Zach held up a charm like the one he'd given me two years ago—this one an owl. "Look at the back."

I took it from him and flipped it over. On the back was a tiny letter Z. Thanking him with a smile, I removed my bracelet and slid the new charm onto the thread, tying knots between it and the rabbit charm.

"Now you have the rabbit with an A for you, and the owl with a Z for me," he said.

"I won't take it off," I promised.

"What's that thing you and Lila do with your pinkies?" Zach asked.

"It's a sort of promise." I crooked my pinkie at Zach. He hooked his pinkie with mine. "We say 'Stay gold' for loyalty and true friendship."

Zach tightened his pinkie around mine. "Stay gold, Amai."

"Stay gold, Zach."

We didn't unhook our pinkies. Zach stared deep into my eyes, and my heart sped up.

"Daisukidesu," he said.

"Yeah," I said, my face burning. "I like you, too, Zach. A lot."

Smiling, he leaned toward me and paused, our noses inches

apart. This time I closed the gap, and we kissed. A real first kiss. Fireworks burst in my chest, throwing off sparks of love and friendship, truth and forgiveness, memories past and memories future. Their warmth would sustain me until the next time we were together.

When we said goodbye in the driveway, Zach and I repeated our promises to stay in touch. And this time, we both meant it. Words and actions could sometimes be misleading, misunderstood, misremembered, but I knew that Zach and I, from this moment on, would try our best to be honest and open.

We'd see each other next summer. Maybe things would be different. Maybe they wouldn't. But we knew we'd be back together to make new memories—amazuppai.

Sweet and sour.

Acknowledgments

This entire book was conceived and written during the COVID-19 pandemic. I was grateful to be able to escape into Mai and Zach's world every day. I am also grateful to many people, including you for reading and sharing my books.

I feel very lucky to call Jenne Abramowitz my editor and friend. She makes me smile and she makes me a much better writer. We have the same (sweet) taste in books and TV, so it's no surprise that we work so well together. Thank you, Jenne! Big thanks also to my agent and friend, Tricia Lawrence, for always being on my side and for making my dreams come true. I'd also like to thank the Erin Murphy Literary Agency for all the support!

Thank you to everyone who provided sweet moments during the writing of this book: Jo Knowles and Cindy Faughnan, my writing partners, for daily check-ins, feedback, and friendship; Kristy Boyce for long conversations about everything including books and writing—you really get me; Susan Tan for writing retreats, get-togethers, and our shared love for all the good food; and Andrea Wang, my soul sister, for encouraging, inspiring, and being there for me. While we had to miss our in-person writing retreat, our virtual retreat helped me get through the first draft. Thanks also to anam cara Lynn Bauer for calls every week over the last nine years and to authors Josie Cameron, Jason June, and Winsome Bingham—your support is priceless. Many thanks to the Highlights Foundation, George Brown, and the incredible staff for providing the perfect writing retreat space and having me on the faculty (another dream come true). Finger hearts and much respect to BTS and ARMY.

A big shout-out to my #AsianAmericanKidLit group—Sarah Park Dahlen, Jung Kim, Betina Hsieh, Mike Jung, Paula Yoo, Minh Lê, and Gene Luen Yang for Zoom gatherings, support and laughter, and text threads that last late into your night so that I wake up to 661 messages.

To Scholastic for making me feel like family. I'm so happy my books have a home with you. Big cheers to Team Sweet and Sour, including Abby McAden, Shelly Romero, Jordana Kulak, Rachel Feld, Janell Harris, Nikki Mutch, Lizette Serano, and Danielle Yadao, and, for an amazing cover, Jacqueline Li, Stephanie Yang, and Yaffa Jaskoll.

Much appreciation to teachers and librarians for reading and sharing books with your students. A special thank-you to Mr. Schu for all the book love—and for photos of my book as you trekked around France.

To the "Lehigh Zoo"—my zoology major college friends, former housemates, and UC Davis Raptor Center colleagues for cheering me on: Diane Kisich Davis, Stephanie Burns, Cicely Muldoon, and Becky Waegell, with a shout-out to Dolly the barn owl. And thanks to the Denison Pequotsepos Nature Center for assistance when I rescued a waterlogged osprey.

During the first sixteen years of my marriage, we moved eight times for my husband's career. It wasn't until we moved to Mystic that we found our home, sweet home. Much appreciation to neighbors, Bill and Nancy, Michael and Christine, Arlene, and Anita and Paula for friendship and community. Love and thanks to Bank Square Books staff present and past including owner, Annie Philbrick; Kelsy; Anastasia; Katie; Doug; Dan; Ruth; Elissa; John (Franny); and Kate. A shout-out to Pamela Zagarenski, the artist who painted the whale sculpture in front of the bookstore. Many thanks to Nana's Bakery and Pizza, including owners, James Wayman and Aaron Laipply; Dave (the bread!!); Corey; Madeline; Peter; and the rest of the talented bakers and staff who keep me well fed. A big shout-out to Rick Koster of the *Day* for taking the time to give my books a shout-out!

And while any errors are mine alone, much appreciation to

expert readers, friends, and family for answering queries, including Gia Pineda and Caitlin Schumacher for BTS references, Junko Mikami for helping with Japanese names and meanings for all my books, and Jerry Craft for answering my questions on life as a graphic novelist. Special thanks to Greg and Jess Andree for allowing me to ask questions of their daughters, Novalee and Willow.

Family is everything to me. There are sweet and sour moments, but there is always love.

My husband, Bob Florence, has supported me through my entire journey to publication, never once losing faith in me and my stories. I could not be here, a published author, without his love and encouragement.

My daughter, Caitlin Masako Schumacher, who, from the time she was a child, always encouraged me to write, pointing out that I got crabby if I didn't write every day, and always believed that I'd make it.

It's tough to truly understand the ups and downs of a writing career, and yet my family always made me feel like I was following a noble path. So much love to Bob; Caitlin; my stepson, Jason Florence; my mom and stepdad, Yasuko and Bob Fordiani; my sister, brother-in-law, and niece, Gail Hirokane, John Parkison, and Laurel Parkison; and to my uncles, aunts, and cousins. And finally, to my late father, Denta Hirokane: I wish you were still around. Thanks for reading to me when I was a child. I miss you and love you.

About the Author

A third-generation Japanese American, Debbi Michiko Florence is the author of *Keep It Together, Keiko Carter* (New England Book Award finalist) and *Just Be Cool, Jenna Sakai* (Amazon Best Books of the Year), as well as the Jasmine Toguchi chapter books. A native Californian, Debbi has called Mystic, Connecticut, home for the last nine years and lives there with her husband, rescue dog, and rabbit. She is ARMY, and J-Hope is her bias. Visit her online at debbimichiko florence.com.